South

Short Stories
Fact, Fiction and Folktales

A Journey Across The Ozarks and Beyond

Best Wishes

The Journey Begins

Ronnie Powell

With special thanks to
Joyce my wife and family,
and of course Polly Anna.

Library of Congress Control Number: 2006906667

ISBN: 0-615-13211-1

First Edition

Additional copies of this book may be purchased by mail at
Cross Road Publication
3 Moon Valley Road
Windyville, Missouri 65783
Or call
417-345-8758
E-mail captredoak@todays-tech.com

Printed in the U.S.A. by
Morris Publishing
3212 East Highway 30
Kearney, NE 68847
1-800-650-7888

Introduction

South Through Barefoot Pass
By Ronnie Powell

Legends, myths and folklore, whispers from the past, perhaps incomplete, faded and often their origins are questionable. They are small aspects of people's lives and events scattered through the aged memories of hand-me-down tales, embellished, recolored and presented often as the absolute truth.

Many tales began as songs or from the sketchy chronicles of diaries or letters; and later a word changed here and there adding color to emphasize a person, place, thing or event. Every story written since man began scratching out images on the walls of caves has later been fortified with other images born of imagination to concoct a story worthy of telling. A seven shot, (Lucky Seven), revolver found frozen in rust lying among the rubble of a moonshine cave, a whiskey bottle hidden behind the wall of a dilapidated cabin containing a swallow or two of the fiery liquid, an old Stetson hat bearing the name of its original owner, rescued from a dusty second hand store are but a few of the artifacts that have inspired this author.

A Tale or Two of U. S. Marshal Edward Hiccup, (And Outlaw Black Jack Ace), is purely fiction as are many of the stories in this book. It is a rowdy comedy of two old men trapped in an 1800's old folks home, yet there is a grain of truth, depicting places, dates and events adding authenticity to the imaginary people portrayed. The Rusty Bucket and Dog Leg Saloons may not have existed but many like them did, scattered throughout the country. They were notorious places, often immoral and lawless.

The Last Osage is a saga pertaining to the final removal of the Osage Indian. It is a fictitious story based on actual events, first written as a living history melodrama and played out before an audience. The actual event took place in the Valley of the Moon, located along the Niangua River in Southern Missouri and represents the last stand of a renegade Osage Chief, Banditti of the Niangua.

The Ghost of Dugan Lane is based on folklore, yet sworn by many to be the truth where a ghost walks along a shadowy lane and some say still does. The tale varied from person to person and the only significant facts in the lore is the location where an old homestead house and well shed stood before they succumbed to fire.

Lalleta's Christmas, is based on and constructed from the authors observations of the plight of homeless people in Mexico City, depicting a young woman amputee and her daughter struggling to survive in the alleys and shadows around the Grand Plaza of the City.

One by one the thirteen stories in this book will take you to places, times and events that are a part of history, viewed though the mind's eye of the author. Humor, adventure, tragedy, hope and faith are the foundation of the tales.

Niangua River Legacy, Cold Seats and Spider Webs and Country Roads are essays revealing the author's appreciation and love of the land, its people and remnants of Americana.

"Adventure lies ahead along the crooked road that slips through Barefoot Pass. Ride easy my friend, watch your top knot and do the best you can.

I have stood numerous times over the years on my journey to distant horizons above Barefoot Pass, watching the morning mist rise from the Niangua River. Each time I could see images floating in the mist and was never certain which one was real and which was imaginary. It is truly a place of mystery and the keeper of many secrets of the past."

Table Of Contents

List Of Photographs

A Tale Or Two of U.S. Marshal Edward Hiccup
(And BlackJack Ace)

The Reunion

The town of Buffalo Head, Missouri located near the west bank of Greasy Creek near the south end of Fifteen Mile Prairie began as a trading post for the Indians. The name for the town came about when in 1858 Tucker Jones arrived by wagon from parts unknown to trade with the Indians, or rather to steal as much from them as he could. An old buffalo skull lying near the trail prompted Tucker to mount it on a post and thus the name Buffalo Head. He hastily constructed a small building of sycamore logs, unloaded the wares he carried and opened the door for business.

The following year Tick Hornsworth arrived at the trading post riding a tall black and tan mule and leading three others loaded with jugs of Tennessee moonshine whiskey. The two men sat for awhile drinking the white lighting, got into an argument over who had drunk more and began slugging it out. Tick whipped Tucker drug him into the Trading Post and left him lying on the floor. Too liquored up to sleep, Tick rode one of the mules to Greasy Creek and spent the next several hours cutting sycamore logs. Morning found Tick asleep on a pile of logs lying next to the trading post.

Both men were a little grumpy to say the least, but after a few swallows of moonshine drippings, they set forth building a saloon and by noon had completed the project. The question arose about what to name the saloon. Tucker suggested calling it the Bear Claw, but Tick said no and again they began to fight. Tucker threw an old bucket at Tick hitting him on the head.

"That's it!" Tick shouted. "Gol-dang it I'll call the saloon the Rusty Bucket."

Not much went on in Buffalo Head for a time, catering to drifters and Indians and an occasional woman of ill repute. The Indians grew tired of being cheated with shoddy merchandise and watered down whiskey and attacked one night with a vengeance bent on taking Tucker and Tick's scalp. They burned the Trading Post. They tried repeatedly to set fire to the Rusty Bucket, but after several braves were shot dead, they gave up and went to Oklahoma; laid claim to a track of land rich in oil. The Indians later returned to Buffalo Head with intentions of buying it, but it stank so bad they left in disgust.

Long about 1860 a circuit riding preacher rode in on a bald faced mare standing eighteen hands high and as skinny as a rail. Tick was standing outside the Rusty Bucket Saloon when Preacher John the Baptist arrived. Tick an animal lover could barely stand to look at the poor mare and went inside and came out with a double barrel shotgun. Not a word he said as he cocked both hammers brought it to bear on the poor critter and pulled both triggers. The mare fell dead in its tracks with the preacher still seated in the saddle.

Preacher John, Tick and Tucker sat for awhile drinking whiskey, discussing the situation rather loudly.

"Preacher," Tucker said, raising his cup. "The Lord works in mysterious ways. I reckon you should build a church."

Preacher John agreed and the three men set forth cutting more sycamore logs and soon it stood on a high knoll a little north of the saloon. Well after that it wasn't long and good honest hardworking folks began arriving. The town began to grow, leaving behind the Rusty Bucket Saloon.

Approximately two years after the Civil War ended, Clara Didwall arrived in Buffalo Head and purchased a house and two acres a little west of the Rusty Bucket. A huge stately house but due to its undesirable location needed paint and repair. The property sat disturbingly close to the Rusty Bucket Saloon, a deplorable place where lay a rather large heap of broken beer bottles and other debris. On the north side of the property set a saw-mill. The noise and dust was a constant irritation. To the east of the property lay open prairie, providing Clara with a little peace and quite.

Clara, heavy with child waddled into town one day with a fist full of posters stating she was available to do house cleaning, laundry and light gardening. She set about placing the posters on fence posts, hitching poles and a couple on the front of the Rusty Bucket Saloon.

Ernestine Didwall began her life toddling around mountains of dirty clothes and wash tubs full of greasy hot water. When barely four years of age she began helping her mother with the washing of other people's clothing and knew little about the outside world. On her twelfth year she asked Clara why she didn't have a father's name. Clara appeared to ponder the question, frowning at her daughter and then answering rather bluntly to never again bring up the subject.

Eighteen years later after a long and painful illness Clara passed away leaving Ernestine quite alone and the heir to the house and two acres. Ernestine armed with the skills needed in washing clothes and gardening and the experience of caring for her invalid mother decided to turn the house into a nursing home for the elderly.

She took inventory of her assets which consisted of thirty seven dollar and fourteen cents. To her dismay she discovered it would take most of the money for a funeral and burial expenses. She decided to forgo a funeral, built a casket from lumber salvaged from and old outhouse sitting near a fence in her back yard and buried her mother in the pit under it.

The Prairie View Nursing Home opened for business less than two weeks following the demise of Clara. After scrounging through the town dump, Ernestine managed to come up with fifteen assorted bed frames, tattered quilts and blankets which she washed and four leaky bed pots. A few days after the opening of the home, it contained twelve decrepit old men placed there by families unwilling to care for them. The fee for housing the men ranged from three to nine dollars a month.

The home was not a fancy place, but clean with each resident provided a bed and three meals a day. The meals consisted of beans and fat back for breakfast, beans and boiled potatoes for lunch and bean broth for supper. Of course there was little to do at the home and most of the old gents sat on the front porch swatting flies and talking about the good old days.

According to many of the town folks in Buffalo Head, no one knew where the stranger came from, arriving late one evening. Most people considered him just another old drunk passing through and not worth a plug nickel. He stumbled into town dog drunk, nearly blind and deaf from years of consuming bad liquor. Tick kicked the old man out of the Rusty Bucket about midnight, followed him to the dilapidated fence at the back of Ernestine's place and threw him over into the yard. The old man curled up on a warm ash pile and went to sleep.

The next morning the fellow awakened, badly needing a drink. Barely able to focus he stood up on wobbly legs mistaking the nursing home for the Rusty Bucket. Smacking his lips in anticipation of a long drought of whiskey he began walking toward the house. He didn't get far and fell face down next to Ernestine's bare feet. He spat dirt along with a bit of an old tobacco cud and looked up. Before him stood a rather tall, heavy hipped woman clothed in a faded feed sack dress. Bright red hair pulled tight into a bun around a wide equally red sunburned face peered down at him through blue eyes.

"Old man you're shamefully drunk," Ernestine scolded.

"Eh what did you say woman?" asked the man.

"I said you are, oh never mind," replied Ernestine. "I think it best you come inside out of the sun for a spell."

The man grunted, managed to get to his feet, but still had to look up at Ernestine. Tugging at the dirty red beard on his chin he frowned and said. "You shore are a tall one. Madam I am a retired United States Marshal and have been taking care of myself long before you were hatched, so don't get all lathered up over my wellbeing. I was just heading for that saloon over there when I stumbled and fell."

Smiling sweetly, Ernestine brushed aside a lock of hair and moved a bit closer to the man. "Oh my goodness you are a real lawman. You must receive a handsome pension for the many brave and gallant years you served. I swear you don't look old enough to retire."

Grinning, the Marshal straightened up, thumbed back a greasy sweat stained hat, then spat tobacco out of one corner of his mouth. "Why thank you Madam," he said, "many a woman has said I look younger than I am. Yes I receive a pension for my years as a marshal, twenty eight dollars a month to be exact."

"Oh my," Ernestine gushed, rapidly blinking her eyes. "I would like to hear more. Please come in and set a spell. I have a pot of beans in the warming oven and a pan of fresh baked cornbread. You are more than welcome to partake of them."

"I don't know Madam," the Marshal said, "I was heading over to the saloon, but heck I sure could eat some of them beans and cornbread."

"Come then, Ernestine smiled, reaching out taking the Marshal by the arm and began pulling him toward the nursing home. "I thought marshals rode horses."

Unable to pull free of the vise like grip, the Marshal trotted along beside her. "They sure do," he grunted. "I lost old Nick about ten miles back. That blame horse stumbled and fell over a bluff and if not for a low hanging limb I would surely have taken the fall with him. Hey slow down a bit."

"Come dear we are about there," Ernestine replied gruffly, pulling the Marshall up the steps of the front porch. "Did the fall kill your horse?"

"Yeah it did," he answered. "When I got down to where he lay several buzzards were sitting on him. Funny thing though they weren't eating on him, but a ripping and tearing at the saddle. I reckon that old horse was just too tough to eat."

Ernestine hooked a big toe in the bottom of the screen door flung it open and shoved the Marshal inside. From there she guided him to a chair near a table and shoved him into it. "I do hope the poor animal didn't suffer much," she said softly."

Rubbing his arm the Marshal glanced toward the door, but remained seated. "I reckon he did, but what bothers me most is what a feller once said to me about Nick."

Smiling, Ernestine pulled the hat from the Marshal's head tossing it into a corner of the room. "And what was it he said?"

A bit distracted by the removal of the hat, the Marshal looked up at Ernestine, before answering. "The feller said Nick wouldn't make good Buzzard bait and dang if he wasn't right."

"My goodness, where are my manners," Ernestine said. "I haven't introduced myself. My name is Ernestine Didwall and I am the proprietor of this well run establishment. What is your name Sir?"

"What did you say?" asked the Marshal, peering into the blue eyes of the woman.

"I said my name is Ernestine and I'm the proprietor of…."

"I heard the rest, but I didn't catch your last…."

"What is your name?" Ernestine demanded.

Leaning forward in the chair, the Marshal spit tobacco down one of his boots. "Well uh, I…." he stammered.

"Come now don't be bashful," Ernestine replied, pushing the Marshal roughly back in the chair.

"My name is Edward Hiccup," said he in a quite voice.

Ernestine's face immediately took on a pale hue and she moved closer. Peering down at Hiccup she began picking at the dead skin on her sunburned nose, saying nothing for a moment or so. Finally she pulled a tuft of hair loose from the bun on the back of her head eyeing it closely and then looked at the hair on the Marshal's head. Nodding grimly, she decided she had the same round face as the man sitting in the chair and the same blue eyes. She sat down.

"Lordy, Lordy," she cried. "Tell me Marshal Edward Hiccup was you ever in Dog Town say thirty years ago?

Fear brightened the normally dull eyes of the old man and he calculated the distance between him and the door and how long it would take him to make it outside. Leaning forward again he spit tobacco down the other boot and then sagged back onto the chair. He knew he could not out run Ernestine. "I don't remember if I was ever in Dog Town," he answered.

Hiccup watched as Ernestine opened a drawer in the table and brought forth an envelope. She removed from the envelope a weathered paper and slowly unfolded it. She looked up through narrowed eyes, staring directly at him. He shrank even further back in the chair, laying a hand on the butt of his Colt Forty Five.

"I have here a letter," Ernestine said quietly. "I found it a few days after Mother's death. It is a love letter or so it appears to Clara Didwall. Did you ever know Clara?"

"Uh, I uh really don't remember," Hiccup replied.

"Oh you don't," Ernestine shouted jumping to her feet. "Well you signed the letter Marshal Edward Hiccup. Clara was my Mother you old fool."

"Oh no," moaned the Marshal.

"Oh yes," Ernestine replied, grabbing a handful of beard pulling Hiccup to his feet. "You're my Pa and danged if you're just gonna leave. That pension of yours is going to come in handy. No you ain't leaving. It's time you faced up to the responsibility of being a parent."

Marshal Hiccup sat with head down considering the situation again eying the door. Looking up into the blue eyes that mirrored his, he shook his head, spitting across the floor. "I ain't staying and that's my final word," he declared.

Tossing the letter on the table, smiling, Ernestine said as gently as if to a baby. "Oh but you will even if I have to tie you up. That pension of yours is going to be compensation for all the years I grew up without a father. If you do escape I will track you down and drag you back here by that tuft of hair you call a beard. You are here to stay for as long as you live and then you will be buried next to Mother. You will abide by the rules. There will be no drinking of alcohol, no swearing and you will bath at least once a week without exception."

"I could just shoot you and walk out of here," Marshal Hiccup said rather timidly.

Eying her father sternly, Ernestine shook a finger threateningly. "If you ever pull that pistol on me Ill take it away from you and you'll never see it again. Is that clear?"

"Yeah, the Marshal muttered. "If I had any doubts about you being Clara's daughter I don't now. I reckon that's the reason I snuck off, the woman was just too durn bossy, about half mean and too big to wrestle."

Standing directly in front of him with hands planted firmly on broad hips and glaring down at him, Ernestine smiled wickedly. Turning she went to the stove, filled a bowl with beans and slid it across the table.

"Bossy or not is not for you to decide, but you're staying and if you try to run, I'll catch you and tie you up like a dog on a leash. Eat those beans and when you're finished go out onto the porch with the rest of our nice guests, swat flies and chaw tobacco. I won't here anymore about it"

The Gunfight

Early the following morning Marshal Edward Hiccup slowly made his way out onto the front porch of the nursing home and sat down in a rocking chair. The face of the old man appeared drawn and bit paler than usual, but the eyes sparkled with defiance. He sat alone watching the sun rise over Fifteen Mile Prairie. After several minutes he cut a chew, tucking it in a gap between his back teeth. Glancing around at the door, he then removed a small brown bottle and took two quick swigs of corn whiskey. He contentedly began rocking back and forth to the rhythm of a boot heel. The dark intensity of the eyes lessoned a bit as he sat reminiscing.

Sighing, the Marshal drank again from the bottle, hiding it in an inner coat pocket. From a worn holster on his belt he removed an ivory handled, Colt forty five revolver, slowly, deliberately bringing up the gun sighting down the barrel, smiling grimly; gently touching a scarred U.S. Marshal's badge pinned to the left lapel of his coat.

Suddenly the screen door burst open, disrupting the golden silence of the morning. Ernestine stood before him dressed in a long white flannel nightgown and barefoot. Her hair unbound hung to her hips, catching the morning sunlight. She held in one hand a steaming cup of tea.

"My goodness dear," she said sweetly, "you're up early. I brought you a cup of tea."

The old man spat a stream of tobacco over the steps, slipped the Colt back into the holster. "I ain't your dear and I don't want a cup of gol-dang tea," he snapped. "I once knew a man who drank tea and the last I heard he was growing lilies and selling them along side the road."

"Oh Pa don't be so stubborn," Ernestine scolded. "Why do you still carry that dreadful gun?"

"Ain't none of your business," he declared.

"But if you have to know I carry it for my protection. I sent a lot of men to prison and you never know when one of them varmints may come looking for me. You ain't getting my pistol!"

"Pa you're too old to be worrying about such things," Ernestine said. "Sheriff Get. A. Long would take care of anyone who might come to Buffalo Head intending to do you harm. The man is fearless. Some folks say he could out gun Jessie James. Now, you drink this tea before it gets cold and I'll be back shortly with your breakfast."

Hiccup reluctantly took the tea, held it at arms length until his daughter went inside and then sat it on the floor. Scowling at nothing in particular, he again removed the brown bottle from the coat pocket drinking the remainder of the whiskey. Slipping the bottle back into the coat he took a deep breath, closed his eyes and pretended to be asleep.

A few minutes later the screen door again swung open. "Pa," Ernestine called out happily, "I forgot to tell you that you now have a roommate. The gentleman was brought in late last night. Wake up now, I want you to meet him."

Wincing at the high pitched voice of his daughter, Hiccup thumbed back the hat, turned to see Ernestine standing next to a tall, bearded old man. A wide brim black hat shadowed the fellow's face, but he could make out dark beady eyes staring back at him. Recognition flashed in the old Marshal's eyes and he jumped straight out of the chair, brandishing the Colt. "Black Jack Ace, you son of a dog is that you?"

Grinning from ear to ear Black Jack lunged forward pulling the tail of his coat back over a holstered revolver. "I'll be danged," he said. "I thought I finished you off for sure at Bear Foot Pass! You shore looked dead."

Hiccup cursed, stepping away from the rocking chair. "Well unless you're blind, you can see I ain't dead you back shooting son of a dog."

"Heck Marshal I shore wish you'd stop calling me a son of a dog," Black Jack replied. "My Pa was a good honest hard working Christian man."

"I reckon," Hiccup said. "I knew your Pa and he was an upstanding feller. But you are a back shooting varmint and we're gonna settle this today. So get your outlaw butt down them steps and get ready to die like a man."

"Boys, boys, Ernestine screamed, "What is going on here?"

Ignoring the distraught woman, Black Jack and Hiccup slowly descended the steps to the ground, turned and faced each other. Ernestine clinging to a porch post continued screaming, forcing the old men further away from the porch.

"Let's shoot her Marshal, put her out of her misery," shouted the outlaw. "I can't concentrate with all that caterwauling and blubbering."

"Naw we can't do that Black Jack," he answered. "The dang woman is my daughter! We'd hang for sure."

Laughing gleefully, Black Jack doubled over. "She's your daughter? That's justice for sure."

"Shut up and stand tall!"

Ernestine exhausted, stood limply against the post staring down at the two men. A clatter of hooves caught her attention; she smiled and waved franticly at a man riding an iron gray mule galloping through the yard gate. The mule came to a sliding halt, braying loudly.

"Sheriff Get. A. Long, please stop those men from shooting each other!" Ernestine cried. "The one on the right is my Pa."

The sheriff a small wry man removed his hat, revealing a lustrous shock of black curly hair. Tossing the hat to the ground the Sheriff dismounted; swaggered toward the two old men and pulled a revolver from his belt. "You gents hold up there. "I ain't gonna have no gun fighting in this town. I reckon I can out gun Jessie James and I see no reason I can't put you old timers in the ground dead and cold."

Paying no attention to the Sheriff, the two men drew their weapons, glaring menacingly at each other. Sadly, years of hard drinking and carousing had dimmed their vision and were unable to see each clearly. Sheriff Get. A. Long fearing for his life ducked but too late for the Marshal fired his weapon, ripping off the hair on top of the Sheriff's head, sending the wig spiraling into the air. Black Jack's revolver roared hitting the left heel of the Sheriff's boot, knocking the fellow off balance.

Ernestine fearing the Sheriff had been mortally wounded leaped off the porch and ran to where he lay.

Again the Marshal squeezed off a shot, oblivious to the drama taking place between him and Black Jack. The bullet finds its mark burning Ernestine's thighs, ripping a jagged hole in the nightgown and cutting a deep furrow in the grass behind her.

"Oh my God I've been hit," she cried, pulling up the gown and then falling across the Sheriff.

"Are you still standing Marshal?" Black Jack drawled peering through the shroud of smoke.

"I sure am Jack Ace," he replied. "I reckon we're just wasting ammunition. "Let's set a spell, I'm tuckered out. I got a little corn squeezing left in a bottle in my room and I'll share it with you."

The Funeral

Marshal Hiccup and Jack Ace were confined under lock and key to their room as punishment for the shooting incident. To add insult to injury their weapons, boots and hats were confiscated and now were locked away in Ernestine's room. Confinement to the small room was especially difficult for the two men, for they were also denied alcohol and chewing tobacco. The Sheriff had not pressed charges; for he and Ernestine were lovers and he chose to tolerate the old gents.

Early on the tenth day of their confinement, Marshal Hiccup sat on a chamber pot, gazing idly about the room. "I'll tell you again like I did yesterday and the day before," grunted Hiccup, "we can't go on living like this. Hogs fare better than we do. They get plenty to eat and drink"

Nodding, Black Jack replied. "Nope we sure can't, but I don't know how we can get out of here. That daughter of yours and that squirrelly Sheriff has the door locked up the same as the window."

"We may die here, Jack Ace."

"That's it!"

"What's it?"

"Awe Hiccup get your butt off the pot, I hate talking to a man when he's taking his morning constitution."

"Well dang it alright," Hiccup replied, pulling up his britches and stepping away from the pot "Now go on and tell me what you're all fired up about."

"Marshal, you and me are gonna die right here this very morning!"

"Is that what you made me get off the pot for? Here it is just barely sunup and you're talking crazy. I ain't got no intentions of dieing in this bug infested room."

"Marshal listen to me, I didn't mean we will actually die, just pretend to."

"Gol-dang, how we gonna do that?"

Obviously pleased with himself, Black Jack grinned rubbing his hands together. "Now you listen. "Are you good at playing dead?"

"Yep I can slobber as good as any dead man," replied the Marshal. "I remember one time over…."

"Shut up we ain't got time for one of your long winded tales. "Just make sure you look dead and rigormortis has set in when the time comes.

"Rigor what?"

"Mortis," replied Black Jack, "it means your stone cold dead and stiff as board. Hurry and get on the bed it's about time for that daughter of yours to bring us our morning beans. I'll fill you in as we go along."

A few minutes later a key rattles the lock in the door and it opens slowly. Ernestine peers inside and then steps quietly into the room. In one hand she balances a tray with two bowls of beans and two cups of coffee. In the other hand she grips a rather large hickory stick. Shaking her head in disgust at the cluttered room and open chamber pot, she hurries to a table near the bed where the old men lay and sets the tray down. She pinches her nose at the foul odor in the room, turning slowly toward the Marshal and Black Jack.

Black Jack lies next to the wall on his back legs spread apart, eyes and mouth wide open. Marshal Hiccup lies on the outside of the bed with one arm dangling over the edge, staring blankly at her, salvia dribbling from his open mouth, staining the pillow and pooling on the floor.

Ernestine anxious to leave the room prods the Marshal with the hickory stick. "Pa get up, come on now quit sulking," she scolded. "I ain't gonna tell you again and I'll walk out of here with your breakfast. Pa, Mister Ace, you get up this minute!"

Stepping closer to the prone figures on the bed, Ernestine closely scrutinizes each face. Taking a deep breath she bends even closer over the Marshal; detects no breathing and steps back. She leans on the stick and stands for a time as if paralyzed.

"Oh lordy I think they're dead," she whispered hoarsely.

Flinging the stick to the floor she began screaming at the top of her lungs, backing slowly out the door.

"Hee, hee," Hiccup chuckled gleefully, "I think we fooled her Black Jack."

"Well it ain't over until they carry our carcasses out of here and plant them in the ground somewhere out back."

"I ain't about to let them put me in the ground," Hiccup said. "Getting put in the ground ain't pretending."

"You danged idiot," Black Jack growled, "they ain't gonna put us in the ground, we'll see to it they think they did. Now lay still because that daughter of yours and the Sheriff will come busting in here any moment."

Sure enough they could here Ernestine squalling for Sheriff Get. A. Long and it wasn't but a moment or so after that the pair entered the room. Still squalling and calling out to the Lord for mercy, Ernestine stood behind the Sheriff. He picked up the hickory stick and began prodding the two men.

"I'm so sorry my darling, but as you suspected the men are dead, he said, patting her on the shoulder.

"Oh dear," she wailed, "poor Pa and Mister Ace. I guess it was their time to go and I can't question the Lord. He knows best. I'm sure of that."

"Yes my dear, he certainly does," replied the Sheriff. "By the way did you take out that life insurance policy on your Pa like we discussed?"

Sniffing loudly, nodding, Ernestine answered. "Yes I did four days ago and I paid a dime more for the maximum benefit amounting to ninety six dollars and sixty seven cents payable on his death certificate."

The sheriff smiled. "You are truly a wonder my love".

"I think we should notify Mister Underhill and have him come and take Pa and Mister Ace to the funeral home," Ernestine suggested, wiping her nose on the hem of her skirt.

The Sheriff shook his head and began stroking Ernestine's unbound hair. "Ernestine do you realize Mister Underhill will charge ten dollars to bury your Pa and Mister Ace and even more if he puts them in a box."

"Oh my goodness!" she cried. "I never thought about that. That is a lot of money. You know, I bet Pa and Black Jack would not want a fancy funeral. They were outdoor men and would probably rather be buried in a blanket."

"I do believe you're right," the Sheriff said smiling. "Don't you think Gunny sacks would be more appropriate to bury them in? Blankets are rather expensive to put in the ground"

"Yes, oh yes you're right," Ernestine cried. "You are such a comfort in my time of grief and uncertainty."

"Thank you. Please if I may, leave everything to me. You go and sit on the front porch while I fetch some gunny sacks from the barn. It won't take long and I'll have the bodies ready for burial and then we'll walk over to the Reverend Straightlace's home and arrange the funeral for the departed."

Who will you get to dig the graves?"

"There are a couple of fellers who hang out at the Rusty Bucket Saloon that will do it for a dollar, especially if we bury them in one hole," the Sheriff replied.

Ernestine looked across the room to the bed where the ridged figures lay. "One hole is enough," she whispered.

"Come now dear, you should leave," the Sheriff said. "It won't be long and the bodies will start grinning and soon after bloating will begin. We must get them in the ground as soon as possible. Sadly there's nothing more you can do for your beloved father and Black Jack."

Marshal Hiccup slowly turned his head toward the door listening. "They are gone Black Jack."

Black Jack snorted. "If that don't beat all," he said. "Sounds to me like a real conspiracy going on, what with the insurance money and all. "It's a wonder they don't just drag us off into the woods and let the buzzards clean our bones."

"I'll be gol-dang!" shouted Hiccup.

"They ain't no use taking it so hard," replied Black Jack."

"No, that ain't it; I could care less about the insurance money and what they've hatched up" laughed Hiccup, "I just remembered something mighty important."

"Are you gonna tell me or not?"

"The night Ernestine brought me in to this room I had three bottles of whiskey, one in each of my boots and another in my coat. I drank one the next morning and we finished the second bottle after the shoot out. The third bottle is hidden under the dang mattress."

"You mean to tell me we suffered the last several days for nothing?" "If I had my pistol I'd shoot you dead."

"Oh quit your whining," laughed the Marshal. "We need it now more than ever. Here you take the first drink old buddy."

Black Jack pulled the cork and drank deeply and then handed the bottle to Hiccup. "Hurry up; the Sheriff will be back anytime to put us in them gunny sacks."

"My lord man you drank near half of it," grumbled Hiccup tipping the bottle up. "Tell me you good for nothing varmint how are we gonna get out of being buried alive?"

Black Jack shook his head frowning. "I don't rightly know," he said. "We need to find something to put in them sacks after the Sheriff leaves. Most important just play dead for the time being and don't blink an eye."

Sheriff Get. A. Long returned shortly humming merrily. Tossing two rather large dusty gunny sacks on the bed he stood back regarding the men. He then pulled both men to edge of the bed and careful not to touch their flesh searched the clothing. Finding nothing of value he rolled the Marshal over and began sacking the old gent. Soon the Marshal disappeared into the confines of the sack. The Sheriff quickly stuffed Black Jack into a sack. Spying the bottle lying on the bed he picked it up, smiled and proceeded to drink the remainder of the fiery liquid. The results sent the Sheriff to his knees as he tried to catch his breath. Gasping, wheezing, he stumbled from the room.

"He's gone," whispered the Marshal. "I can hear him out on the porch gagging like an old hound sick on bad opossum." The whiskey was too much for that sorry excuse of a man."

Black Jack's head appeared, covered in dust and remnants of chicken feathers. "Dang, I about strangled to death," he said. "I reckon the dust got to the Sheriff too. Come on let's get out of the sacks and try to find something to fill them with."

"Like what," wheezed the Marshal?"

"I don't know, but first I got to have a drink to clear my throat," said Black Jack. "Well shoot me in the butt, that dandy of a sheriff done and drunk all our whiskey!"

"Never mind the whiskey," Hiccup declared. "I just thought of how we can fill them sacks. There are two halves of sugar cured hog a hanging in the pantry. They will be about right, stiff as a board they are."

"Splendid," Beamed Black Jack. "Let's get on with it."

Less than twenty minutes later the remains of the hog lay on the bed enclosed in the two sacks. Marshal Hiccup and Black Jack stood by admiring their handy work.

"Look at them Marshal how the leg on one pooches out. Rigormortis has set in or so it will appear to Ernestine and the Sheriff. Do you reckon that old man we came up on in the hall will tell on us?"

"Naw he won't I think he's plotting to kill Ernestine," replied the Marshal. "Black Jack you go and stand at the window to make sure our funeral party don't slip in on us. I'm going to Ernestine's bedroom and fetch our belongings and then we can hide in the closet until dark."

The first through the bedroom door strode Reverend Straightlace, followed by his wife Gertrude. Next came Ernestine bawling loudly, followed by the Sheriff. The Reverend a tall boney man with large hands and feet stood next to the bed decked out in a black suit. He motioned for all to gather round as he opened the Bible. The preacher uttered a short prayer followed by silence.

"Dearly beloved we are gathered here today to pay homage to the departed father of Ernestine Didwall", began the Reverend in a slow monotonous voice. "Next to him lies a fellow by the name of Black Jack Ace. I am told that both of these men were of questionable morals. Blessed are the meek for they shall enter Heaven's door, but I fear these two wretched souls will be turned away. When the roll is called up there they won't be there, they won't be there. Amen."

"Amen," replied the others

.The Sheriff with bowed head pressed a dollar bill into the preacher's out stretched hand. "Those were fine words Sir," said he. "We must get the bodies to grave side, for as you can see rigormortis has set in."

Shouldering the sacks containing the hog halves were difficult and both men staggered under the awkward load. Sweating profusely they arrived at the grave site and heaved the sacks into the hole. Two men obviously drunk stood leaning on shovels, grinning from ear to ear.

"You fellers didn't get the hole very deep," said the Sheriff.

One of the men answered. "Deep enough a hound or opossum ain't gonna dig them up."

There is nothing more beautiful or tranquil than a sunset over Fifteen Mile Prairie especially on a summer evening. There is something intriguing about the freedom of the prairie stretching out beckoning to those with wanderlust and so it was as two ragged figures slipped out the back door of the Prairie View Nursing Home and made their way to a mound of dirt near the rear of the building.

"I reckon we're at peace now," muttered Marshal Hiccup.

Black Jack kicked a clump of dirt, spiting tobacco across the grave. "I wouldn't know," he said. "I ain't ever been at peace. I sure wish we had some money."

"Well," the Marshal chuckled, "wishes do come true. I have here in my hand one hundred and twenty dollars I took from under Ernestine's mattress."

Black Jack stood dumb struck staring at the money and then looked up smiling. "Praise be, miracles do happen," he said.

Ducking under the sawmill fence, grinning from ear to ear," Marshal Hiccup said. "Come on you mangy outlaw, let's get out of here. I still ain't forgot how you back shot me and I reckon we're gonna have to settle the score. You ain't nothing but a back shooting son of a dog."

"Awe Marshal don't go talking about my Pa again," Black Jack replied. "God rest his soul, he did the best he could raising me. It wasn't my upbringing that caused me to go wrong. White Lightening whiskey is the reason I became an outlaw.

"I'm sorry, didn't mean any disrespect to your Pa," said the Marshal, shedding a lone tear.

"I'll tell you something Marshal," Blackjack replied, and you probably ain't gonna like it. You ain't no better than me a drinking and cussing like you do."

"Let's it be friend," Hiccup grinned. "I'm in no mood for fighting, maybe another time."

"I got a jug of fine Tennessee whiskey hidden in a hollow tree at Bare Foot Pass," said Black Jack. "Let's head that way."

"Yahoo!" cried Marshal Hiccup. "If we hurry we can be there by morning!"

THE END

Lalleta's Christmas

Lalleta, a young Indian woman and five year old daughter Celina sat huddled together on a straw matt in the entrance way to an ally in the Great Plaza of Mexico City, near the Hotel Emporia. A double amputee from the knees down Laleta held tightly to Celina, watching a group of boisterous Christmas Holiday tourists about to board a bus sitting at the curb.

Two years earlier while on board another bus with her husband and Celina during a rare outing to Salito the unthinkable happened. No one knows for certain why the old bus careened off the mountain highway and plunged down a steep embankment and came to rest in a ravine. Lalleta could hear many of the people crying, moaning begging to be rescued. Lying several feet from the battered bus, Lalleta could barely move and thought it strange she could not feel her legs. Somehow she began crawling up a steep incline toward the wreckage, franticly calling out to Celina. The accent up the slope was especially difficult, again and again slipping back in the blood trail left by the stumps of her legs. Determined to find Celina and her husband, Lalleta slowly advanced nearer the bus. She found Celina first, sitting beside a twisted portion of the vehicle unharmed and then she saw her husband's lifeless body lying under the jagged metal.

Unable to care for herself and Celina, the pair quickly became a burden to family barely able to care for themselves. "Go to Mexico City, for beggars do well there," they assured her. "Tourists will give you many Pecos and soon you will have enough money to return to the mountain."

Several weeks later with just enough money for bus fare and meager food, Lalleta and Celina boarded a bus for Mexico City. The journey was exhausting to say the least and they arrived late in the evening on the second day. Never had she seen such an expanse of people, automobiles and madness that lay before them. Frightened, confused, cold and hungry they took refuge in an abandoned automobile.

Lalleta and Celina wandered aimlessly during the following

days working their way deeper into the city. Binding her bloody hands with cloth torn from her skirt, Lalleta kept scooting along on a board, receiving a Pecos now and then from a kind stranger. Finally after more than a week they reached the Great Plaza, taking refuge deep inside an ally, not far from the Emporia Hotel. They found little comfort there, for they quickly discovered the alleys were infested with rats. Fearing for Celina's safety Lalleta held her close every night. Hope of returning home to the mountains slowly faded from her consciousness.

Wearily Lalleta pushed away from the wall and began calling out for Pecos while holding out a small earthen jar, shaking it vigorously. Celina still wrapped in her night blanket stood up gazing intently at the group of people loitering next to the bus. Reaching out with her free hand, Lalleta pulled the little girl down onto her lap. Scooting further out onto the sidewalk she shook the jar violently calling out again and again for coins.

A dapperly dressed Mexican man stepped jauntily from the bus, smiled and then cheerfully addressed the expectant tourists. Waving a disapproving hand toward Lalleta, he curtly advised them not to give money to the many beggars they would encounter through out the day, for such a practice would result in great inconvenience to them. Smiling, stepping aside the guide motioned for the people to begin boarding the bus.

Lalleta upon hearing the words of the young guide, deliberately moved closer pleading for coins. A tall red headed man wearing fancy western boots stepped away from the line of people to where Lalleta sat. Smiling, he looked down into the dark pleading eyes. Returning the smile Laleta held up the jar. The man thrust a hand into a pocket of his jeans removing several coins, dropping them into the jar. He turned then under the stern eyes of the guide and entered the bus.

Scooting back against the wall next to an old wagon they had found in the ally and now containing their possession, Lalleta watched in silence as the bus pulled away. Tipping the jar she watched several coins spill out onto her hand. She quickly counted the coins and although the red headed man had been generous, there were barely enough to feed them for a couple of days. Shaking her head sadly Lalleta began weeping.

Tossing the blanket on the wagon, kneeling, Celina asked. "Why are crying Mama? What is the matter?"

"Oh it's nothing child," replied Lalleta. "Look we have Pecos. Tomorrow is Christmas and we will buy something special to eat."

Celina too shook her head sadly and then moved closer and began gently smoothing back her mother's hair. "I will get us more Pecos, I promise!"

"No child," Lalleta scolded softly. "Please sit down, for it is not for you to be concerned about. God is watching us and will provide our needs and much more. Please do not worry. You must have faith little girl."

Reluctantly Celina sat down looking up the street. "Mama may I go and look at the beautiful senorita doll in the window of the toy store?" she asked. "I wish you could see it. It has dark eyes and hair and is wearing a white dress."

"Oh I don't know Celina. "I fear for your safety when you go off alone."

"Mother it's not far and I will return quickly," she said. "Please may I go? I will stand at the window and pray that I will receive the doll on Christmas Morning. I have never seen anything as beautiful as that doll."

"Promise me you will not talk to strangers nor walk too close to the street?"

"Yes Mama I promise!" Celina said laughing gleefully. "I will return very quickly."

Lalleta avoiding the bright eyes of her daughter pretended to look down at the jar and only when Celina hurried away did she look up. She watched the small girl until she disappeared into a group of people. She removed from the wagon a tattered cloth bag, taking from it a comb and small mirror and began combing out the tangles in the shoulder length dark hair. She looked into the mirror shaking her head disapprovingly and then tossed it onto the wagon. Tears again clouded the eyes; angrily wiping them away turning her attention to the street to where Celina would come.

Several moments passed as Lalleta waited for her daughter's return and then she saw her walking slowly along the outer edge of the street. She appeared preoccupied with head down walking dangerously close to the traffic rushing past her. It was only when Celina stood before her at arms length did she dare draw a breath of relief.

"Mama," Celina wept, throwing herself into her mother's arms, "the senorita doll is no longer in the window."

"Oh my goodness baby," Lalleta whispered. "Hush now, hush, I told you it wouldn't be there long."

"They even chased me away from the window and told me not to ever come back" she sobbed. "Christmas is not for children like me."

"No!" scolded Lalleta, holding the weeping girl tighter. "You must not say that. We must be thankful for the Pecos we have and I promise we'll have a feast tomorrow."

"Oh Mother I wanted that doll so very bad," cried Celina.

"Put your feet under the blanket and no more fretting. Only God knows what blessing the day will bring us."

Not long before sunset, evening shadows began creeping out of the allies along the streets. The shop windows took on a bright cheery glow and around the Plaza the festivities of Christmas Eve began. Lalleta and Celina sat huddled together partially hidden from view in a narrow service passage adjacent to the Emporia Hotel. They had received no others coins during the day. Holding Celina lovingly to her breast, Laleta watched in silence the people passing by. No one seemed to notice them as they rushed about laughing and singing.

Night had fallen over the city when the charter bus carrying the holiday tourist pulled up along the curb and came to a halt. The arrival of the bus startled Lalleta, but she immediately began shaking the jar calling out for coins. The Tourists, eager to be inside the hotel paid little attention to her, hurrying past without dropping one coin into the jar. One of the last to leave the bus was the red headed man wearing the fancy boots, but he too hurried away and quickly disappeared into the brightly lit interior of the hotel.

"Oh Fancy Boots we need more Pecos," Lalleta called out.

Retreating further into the ally, Celina lead Laleta to a shallow alcove of a boarded up door. She took from the wagon a rather large wool Indian blanket one of but few items that had accompanied them to Mexico City. She laid it down and helped her mother upon it. Shivering she sat down on her mother's lap, pulling the blanket completely over them. Snuggling deep into her mother's arms she lay silently weeping. Sleep came at last for both of the lonely souls, blotting out for a time the bleak existence befallen them.

Church bells across the city began ringing at midnight announcing Christmas morning. Lalleta awakened by the bells leaned back against the boarded up door, tucking the blanket tighter around them. She sat for time after the bells ceased their chiming staring blankly at the dark images of discarded crates and other debris scattered along the narrow passage. Refusing to think about the approaching dawn she closed her eyes and again fell asleep.

A short time later she again awakened, but did not know why. She peered around into the shadows and near the entrance saw the silhouette of a man moving slowly toward them. Too frightened to cry out she instinctively held Celina closer. Wide eyed she watched as the man approached them. He knelt down in front of her and thumbed back his hat and smiled.

"Fancy Boots," she cried, holding out the small earthen jar suddenly recognizing the red headed man.

Nodding, Fancy Boots gently took the jar from her hand and set it down on the wagon. "No that's not necessary Lalleta," he said. "I have more than coins to give you."

Unable to understand all the words he spoke, Lalleta shrank back in fear.

"Please, don't be afraid," the man said. "I want you to have this money. There is nearly five hundred dollars here and it is yours. Do you understand?"

Too stunned to speak, Lalleta could only nod as she felt the money being pressed into her outstretched hand. Fearing he might change his mind she thrust it down the front of her dress.

"I talked to the old man down the street who has the burrito stand and he told me why you came to this city," he said. "I came to have a good time and decided I have no business spending all this money foolishly when you have so little. "I'm leaving this morning, going back home to my home in Missouri. Lalleta return to the mountains!"

Awed by what she had understood and the reality of the money lying against her breast, Lalleta could only nod and smile.

"Oh," the man said, removing something from his coat placing it next to Celina. "It is the senorita doll Celina so admired. "Please give it to her when she awakens."

Fancy Boots stood up and once again the face was but a shadow. He turned abruptly and walked out onto the street to a waiting cab.

There is an old bus that makes daily runs from Salito to the many small villages scattered along the mountain road. These villages lie several miles north of Mexico City; and represent many descendants of the once great Mayan.

Sitting close together on one particular run up the mountain, Lalleta and Celina gaze out the window smiling, anxiously awaiting their return home while Celina holds in her arms the senorita doll

THE END

Author's rendition of a Sioux Chief

The Last Osage

Captain Butcher Redoak stepped out onto a balcony above the compound of Fort Niangua, a freshly lit cigar clamped tightly between his teeth. The September dawn a distant hue on the horizon.

Captain Butcher Redoak a veteran of the Civil War and one of many soldiers participating in the removal of Indians across the Midwest appeared to others in his command as intolerant of the hardships of the Native Americans. He carried out orders without question, often instrumental in running down lone braves refusing to leave the Ozarks along the flood plain of the Niangua and frequently hanging them by the neck until dead. But each time an Indian died or was mistreated the Captain became less eager to follow the next order.

Leaning heavily against the railing, looking down at nothing in particular Captain Redoak a tall red headed, fair skin man, tried to come to terms with an order he had received the day before. The order had arrived in the form of a written communiqué, ordering the final removal of a small renegade band of Osage Indians from the upper portion of the Niangua River basin.

Most of the Osage had been driven out of the Ozarks by the late 1870's and relocated in Oklahoma, however, there was one Indian known as Lone Eagle who refused to leave, eluding Missouri State Militia troops time and again. Sixty other braves managed to sneak back in and joined Chief Lone Eagle. They became known as the Banditti of the Niangua, stealing cattle, horses and occasionally harassing the farmers. Many of the populace demanded their removal.

The Captain, aware of the Indians determination to remain in their ancestral land knew without a shadow of doubt that it would not be easy to persuade this particular group of natives to leave Missouri and was certain there would be bloodshed. For the first time in the ten years he had served in the militia he harbored a growing resentment at being responsible for the plight of the Indians along the Niangua River.

Angrily he flung the communiqué over the railing, watching it spiral down into the compound, the blue eyes flashing defiantly. Wearily he turned, entered his quarters and stood for a time in thought. Tossing the cigar into a chamber pot, he quickly donned a blue frock coat, black hat and stomped down the narrow steps leading to a small office.

Sergeant Ira Ikerred strode from his quarters closely scrutinizing the drab scene around him. Sun bleached auburn shoulder length hair and mustache obscured the weathered face of the lean man. The pale blue eyes and quick sense of smell missed nothing. Grunting he turned and hurried toward the cook shack, well aware of what breakfast would consist of, fat back bacon, sour dough biscuits and coffee as black as ink.

"Sergeant." an impatient voice hailed from the porch of the offer's quarters.

Stopping abruptly turning, Ira threw up a hand. "Yes Sir, what can I do for you Captain Redoak?"

"If the coffee is hot and drinkable, bring two cups to my office, pronto."

"Yes Sir, but I doubt if you could call it drinkable," answered the Sergeant.

To Ira Ikerred pronto meant ducking an arrow met for him or riding hard to cut off the enemy and so he did not consider fetching coffee for the Captain a priority. Ten minutes later he entered the Captain's office to be met with a frown and shake of the head. He carefully slid one of the cups across the desk and sat down in a chair. Grinning he said. "The coffee is as thick as river mud and about as rank."

"That ain't no surprise," replied the Captain, inserting a cigar between his teeth. "Ira do you think Lone Eagle can be persuaded to leave the river peaceably?"

"No," Ira answered abruptly. "Have you got another one of those cigars?"

Frowning, the Captain tossed a cigar across the desk. "Do you have any suggestions on how to handle Lone Eagle and prevent blood shed?"

"No Sir I don't," he answered. "It is my opinion he would rather die than leave his birth place."

"I can't say I blame him, so he may have to die."

Nodding in agreement, Ira replied. "That's a real possibility."

Whether I like it or not I have to follow orders," The Captain said.

"Perhaps you could give him one more chance, talk to him man to man. Allow him to tell you what he's intending to do, and maybe you can reason with him."

"Do you know where the renegades are camping?" asked the Captain.

Ira appeared to give thought to the question gazing out the door. "Two days ago they were camped in Moon Valley. I went there after a farmer living on the north bend of the Niangua complained about one of his heifers gone missing. He did not see the heifer taken, but was certain the Indians were responsible. I managed to get close enough to Lone Eagle's camp to try to prove or disproved the allegation. All I saw were two deer carcass hanging from a tree in the center of the camp. I can't say for sure whether the Indians stole the heifer or not."

"It doesn't matter, take the Delaware breed we have living here in the fort and find Lone Eagle," replied the Captain. "I'm reasonably certain the breed can be trusted. Tell Lone Eagle I want council with him tomorrow about sundown. Tell him to be alone as I will. I will meet him on that high knoll directly below the Hilderbrand cave."

The Sergeants eyes slowly shifted from his cigar to the Captain's face. "You ain't going alone are you?" he asked.

"No, nor will Lone Eagle. That wife of his goes wherever he does."

"What if he doesn't agree to leave peacefully?"

"You're the best shot in the fort," the Captain replied. "Can you kill him at thirty yards in half light?"

"Yes, but…."

"No buts. "If and when I remove my hat take him out," said the Captain.

"Yes Sir."

Lone Eagle sat a short distance from a canvas covered lodge gazing into the glowing embers of a fire. Long gray black hair lay in a single braid across one shoulder; the grim gaunt face reflecting the glow of embers before him. A stone pipe containing tobacco lay nearby and next to it sat an earthen bowl of red haw paste. A woman holding a large knife stood behind him in the door of the lodge.

"Surely my husband you do not trust Captain Redoak?" questioned the woman."

"It is not your place to ask me such a question Yellow Bird," replied Lone Eagle. "Remain in the lodge; I am the one he wishes to talk to."

"You told him you would be alone," she replied.

"I am alone with my woman, now go inside."

Lone Eagle had reluctantly agreed to set in council with the Captain and sent his followers to a high ridge above Moon Valley, too far away to pose any danger to the Captain.

The hills around the pair darkened as night shadows crept up from the river. Lone Eagle sat in silence listening, occasionally glancing up at the blood red sky. The dark eyes of the man appeared to dance in anticipation of the unknown drawing closer to the camp. The faint clatter of hooves caught his attention and then the sound of muffled voices coming from a willow break further down the hill.

Three men emerged from the willows. Two were carrying torches, one a rifle and stopped about thirty yards from where Lone Eagle sat. The tallest of the trio continued on up the hill, stopping beneath the low bows of a hickory tree adjacent to the camp. The man hesitated momentarily and then slowly walked past Lone Eagle to the door of the lodge.

"You're late Captain and you come like a thief in the night," said Lone Eagle.

Pulling aside the flap covering the door, peering into the shadowed interior of the lodge, the Captain came face to face with Yellow Bird. Turning he looked down at the Indian. "I sent word we would meet about sundown," he replied.

"The sun is no longer in the sky," said Lone Eagle. "You brought others with you Captain. We agreed to meet alone."

"Neither one of us kept our word." There is a woman inside your lodge holding a knife."

"Are you afraid of an old woman?" Lone Eagle smiled.

"No not as long as I know where she is," replied the Captain. "Enough of this banter Lone Eagle."

"I will not sit in council with you if the others are to join us," Lone Eagle said.

Dropping to his knees in front of the Indian, facing the front of the lodge, Captain Redoak regarded the Indian closely. "The men will remain where they are."

Nodding, Lone Eagle carefully picked up the stone pipe. Plucking a small glowing ember from the fire placing it into the bowl of the pipe and began drawing deeply on the long sumac stem. Soon fragile wisps of smoke drifted up from the pipe, disappearing into the wind as quickly as they appeared. The Indian continued puffing on the pipe for a time, fanning the smoke skyward. Smiling, Lone Eagle held the pipe out to the Captain and grunted.

"No I did not come here to smoke a pipe," the Captain replied gruffly. "I came here to try and convince you to leave the river and join the rest of your people in Oklahoma. You may not believe this, but it grieves me to tell you that you cannot stay here. The land no longer belongs to you. I'm sure I would feel the way you do if someone told me to leave, but you don't have a choice. I have more soldiers than you do braves and more guns. My chief has ordered me to sit in council with you. Oklahoma belongs to the Indian, not the land along the Niangua River"

Lone Eagle laid the pipe aside, staring defiantly at the Captain; the dark eyes sparkling in the fire light.

"My chief sends a message," the Captain continued. "Many times he has asked you to leave and many times you have refused. There will be no more talk after this council. There will be no more warm blankets for cold winter nights, or cloth for your squaws. I did not come here to deceive you, but to try and reason with you. Whether you like it or not, the white man now owns all the land along the river. The high ridges, hollows and river land no longer will be inhabited by the Indian."

"Captain you did come here to talk, but to make demands," Lone Eagle replied. "Yes, I have heard the words of your chief and they faded from my mind like the morning dew. I do not heed the words of a thief and liar!"

"Lone Eagle, listen!"

"No!" Lone Eagle shouted. "You listen to my words for they will not fade. This land along the river you call Niangua, is the resting place of our ancestors. It is the place of life for us and yes death."

Stunned by the cutting defiant words of the Chief," the Captain rocked back on his heels. Darkness was fast approaching the camp. Below him flames leaped high from the torches held by Ira and the Delaware.

"Captain I will not lead my people from their land!"

Still shaken by Lone Eagles refusal, the Captain stumbled angrily to his feet. "Because of your stubbornness many of your people may die."

"Then better we die," Lone Eagle replied softly. "We are not leaves to tumble in the wind when your Chief blows. We will not lie in a pigsty you call a reservation to suffer and die like dogs on a chain."

Unguarded admiration flashed across the Captain's face and he nodded. "We have nothing more to say to each other," he whispered hoarsely.

Thrusting a hand deep into the red haw paste, Lone Eagle slowly drew the hand down each cheek, leaving a blaze of red. He stood up, turned toward the distant ridge where his followers awaited him. The Indian crossed his arms defiantly, a shadowy figure standing as still and inanimate as a stone.

Captain Redoak moved away from the fire slowly removing the dusty hat from his head followed by the deafening roar of Ira Ikerred rifle shattering the silence of the evening, resounding against the bleak hills around them. Stumbling backward dropping to his knees, Lone Eagle uttered not a sound and fell face down near the stone pipe.

"Captain, you better get on down here," Ira shouted.

"Yeah I'm coming," he answered, running down the hill.

Yellow Bird slowly pushed aside the door flap of the lodge, hesitated then quickly ran to where Lone Eagle lay. Dropping to her knees she pulled the lifeless man across her lap and began chanting a death song. The mournful cry reverberating against the night cloaked hills was soon joined by others chanting from a high distant ridge.

Sitting astride their mounts, the soldiers below the camp listened grimly.

"Let the rest of Lone Eagles people grieve tonight," Captain Redoak said. "Bring them all in at first light by whatever means it takes."

Shouldering the long rifle, Ira answered. "Yes Sir, but I think it was wrong killing that man the way I did."

"Don't worry about it," replied the Captain. "I gave him a choice. Right or wrong it's done. You bear no blame and were following orders."

"He had no choice in the matter," Ira said. "The Indian was dead before we arrived."

"I disagree," stated the Captain and spurred his mount forward. "It's over now, live with it."

"Maybe, maybe not," Ira replied

THE END

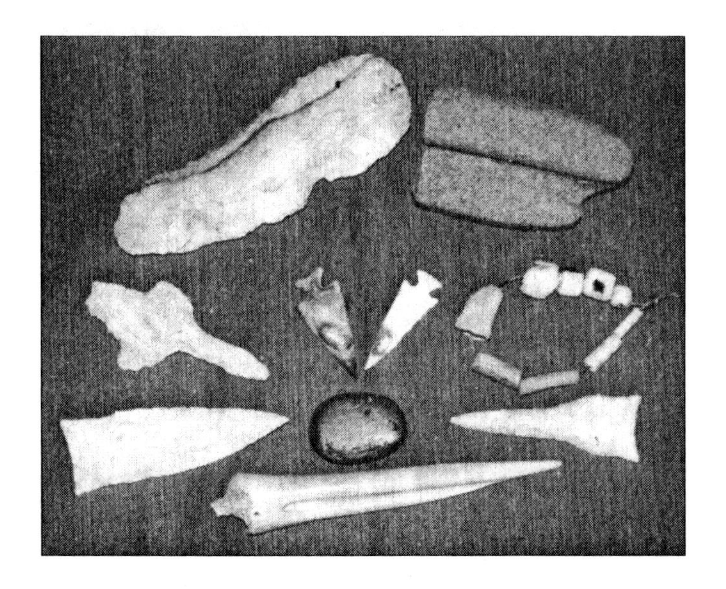

Prehistoric artifact of the Niangua River

Niangua River Legacy

The Niangua River rises from its cradle in Marshfield, Missouri located in Northern Webster County, flows northward into Dallas County, meandering past a vast array of rugged hills, ridges, hollows and limestone bluffs. The River flows from Dallas County into Camden County and finally buries itself in the Niangua Arm of the Lake of the Ozarks. The direct distance overland, or as the crow flies from Marshfield to the burial of this river is approximately 45 miles. But follow the Niangua as it travels its sinuous course and it will take you one hundred forty miles. To fully appreciate the track of the Niangua is to physically experience the wandering of this ancient river. In reality it is a winding stream, snaking its way along the base of many ridges, bluffs and fertile bottom fields. It is erratic in its travel, bending, doubling back and forth, following its only course of exit toward every point of the compass. Truly a serpentine river, the Niangua is with out question a beautiful natural treasure that has suffered greatly since the coming of the white man.

There is a portion of the Niangua River beginning at the Missouri, Highway K Bridge, near Windyville and is a long day's float to the south entrance of the Valley of the Moon, or as it is called today, "Moon valley." It flows along the north face of McKee Ridge, slowing at times in deep, blue green eddies. This aspect of the river when viewed from a canoe drifting with the current can provide an appreciative soul, majestic splendor of natural wonder and an eco system that has long since prevailed in the Missouri Ozarks. The journey should begin at sunrise, or just before and it makes no difference whether it's a gray, misty dawn, or one clear and bright.

Towering limestone bluffs, their faces cracked, harried by perhaps millenniums of weather storms and land upheavals. They are the keepers of many secrets that at times startle even man of the present. Often in the hot muggy days of August, gar fish can be seen lying near the surface of the river, images of another time veiled in a distant horizon. In the dark shadows along the banks, beaver, muskrat and otter abound in this mysterious realm and overhead Bald Eagles set waiting in trees. It is not uncommon in the first flush of dawn to see several buzzards sitting on the limbs of snags, wings outstretched in a ritual as old as the valley itself. These silent sentinels are drying their wings, soon to ride the wind above the river and beyond.

To, many people who pass through the Valley of the Moon, it is just a place to launch a canoe, swim or fish. I think most never fathom the remaining ageless beauty that exists there and most certainly do not appreciate the crumbling remnants of another people and time. Sadly, most of the caves leading into and in the Valley of the Moon bear graffiti and other damage put there by careless hands, and sometimes there are weekend floaters who disrupt the solitude of the river, leaving behind cans and bottles to distort and mar this beautiful stream. I cannot comprehend such drunken expeditions. Yet if one looks close on a quite misty morning there is still a bit of the pristine beauty once prevalent along the length and breadth of the Niangua.

Early one particularly cold November morning many years ago, I began a preliminary journey at the Windyville Bridge down the Niangua River. A journey that lasted more than twenty years detoured at times, ending high on top of a Mayan Pyramid of the Sun, deep in the interior of Old Mexico, above the ruins of a grand city. I braced the wind and too saw the sun glinting off Spanish Armor, moving slowly, relentlessly toward the city and its demise.

In late summer of 1969 I began at the Windyville Bridge to purposely and diligently explore McKee Ridge, a great land protrusion bordering the south bank of the Niangua. High bluffs, deep hollows and ravines abound eastward, ending at the north entrance to the Valley of the Moon. Confident I would find traces of the Prehistory Indians along the way.

A little more than a mile from the bridge I discovered a small bluff, broken in places like the ruins of an old castle. The main body of the bluff sat about two hundred yards above the flood plain of the river and I speculated the bluff had always been above flood stage. The bluff located up a steep incline was not an easy find and is impossible to see from the river. A huge chunk of the bluff lay at its base and appeared to be a part of an old overhang that once jutted out from the bluff.

I began the arduous climb up the hill avoiding patches of briars, but was forced to pass through one especially wide thicket of the prickly growth. Heavily laden with a backpack I soon stopped to rest, hampered by the brush and steep incline. Resting only a moment or so I struggled on toward the bluff, unaware of danger lurking ahead.

The first inclination of danger nearby came when several red wasps darted up out of the thicket and I foolishly paid them no mind. I had moved only a few feet when I glimpsed a large nest to my left. Too late I tried to retreat for the backpack became entangled in the briars and then brushed against the heavily fortified nest. The wasps came at me with surprising speed and accuracy hitting the pack first and then my face neck and hands. Dropping to my knees I quickly shed the pack, removing the bedroll and crawled under it. Hundreds of wasps descended on me and I could hear them hitting the blanket, stinging my exposed hands and arms. Soon the ground swarmed with the defenders of the nest and fearing I might be stung to death began crawling up the slope as fast as I could. My left hand hit especially hard began swelling within seconds of my retreat. It was not until I had put approximately twenty yards between me and the nest the attack lessoned in intensity. I took cover behind an old stump and immediately began raking dry leaves into a pile, setting it afire, adding fuel as the flames grew stronger. I lay in a small clearing about seventy yards from the west end of the bluff, but too afraid to move, I lay under the blanket for a time.

Finally I sat up fanning the smoke watching the wasps diving about and then they were gone. I could feel my face swelling, closing the nose and left eye. The pack lay about half way down the slope and summoning courage took advantage of the shroud of smoke, ran to it and back up the hill, stumbling like a sailor on the high sea. I made a paste of pipe tobacco, powdered sulfur and crushed aspirin spreading it liberally across my face, hands and arms and then swallowed four aspirins. Whether it helped or not I began feeling a little better and lay down. Nauseated by the thirty odd stings I considered trying to get to my car, parked on the road side well over a mile away, but decided to remain on the ridge.

A couple of hours later I awakened from a stupor and sat up. Surprisingly I felt much better although I must admit not fit. The hand appeared strutted beyond belief, radiating pain with each heartbeat and most certainly non functional, yet I considered myself lucky and decided to spend the night at the base of the bluff and not chance a foolish trek up the river.

I gave no more thought to leaving the bluff, determined to stay the night and removed a thermos from the pack and poured a cup of coffee and awkwardly tamped tobacco into my pipe and then sat back to smoke and gather strength for the final leg up the hill to find shelter for the night.

Later that afternoon I shouldered the pack and bedroll and with the sun hovering over the western horizon, I slowly walked up the slope to a portion of the bluff where an overhang protruded that would provide some cover for the night. Dropping the pack I began raking leaves out of the shelter and managed to dig a shallow fire pit. I wanted only to lie down, but decided to build a fire and prepare a meal of canned stew and fried biscuits.

Evening shadows began creeping up the hill soon after finishing the meal and I brought in more wood for the night. The food seemed to have given me a new lease on life and I leaned back against the bluff to at last rest my wounded body.

I awakened at first light a bit stiff and sore from my ordeal. . Every joint ached, but I refused to lie still and got to my feet grunting I suppose like a bear just out of a hibernation cave. I stoked the fire, dug a towel out of the pack and struck out a little southward to a spring I had once visited. The longer I walked, the better I began to feel, yet still very much aware of the massive swelling on my face and left hand.

I found the spring with no difficulty, but it had been reduced to a trickle. Not far below the spring hidden beneath a mantle of fern I discovered a small pool of water quite cool and clear. I filled both canteens and for the best part of an hour knelt there washing my wounds. The water cooled the feverish skin and even reduced the swelling in the left eye. I headed back, watching chipmunks and squirrels playing about on the forest floor and truly glad to be on the ridge.

After returning to camp and feeling much better, I set about making breakfast which consisted of two hardboiled eggs, a baked potato and a pan of fried biscuits. As I sat eating I noticed what appeared to be a hole at the base of the bluff a few feet beyond the overhang. The opening appeared rather small, perhaps too small for me to enter, but intrigued by it I hastily abandoned the meal and with a flashlight in hand went to have a second look. I cautiously approached the opening, recalling past encounters with skunks, foxes, snakes and a crippled buzzard. The beam of the light cut through the darkness within the mouth of the small cave revealing a large cavern that appeared to extend deep inside the bluff. It was evident that at some point in time dirt and stone had slid from somewhere above and partially blocked the entrance, creating a base for other debris to collect there. I immediately began pulling the loose material away until the entrance was large enough to enter. Hurrying back to camp I picked up the pack containing a small pick, garden trowel, a box screen, magnifying glass and other assorted items including spare batteries. I quickly downed two aspirins and hurried back to the cave.

Bending low I entered the cave to find a high ceiling and a cavern at least twenty feet wide and perhaps forty or more feet long. The area was dry, very dry for with each step, dust rose clouding the air behind me. Near the center of the cavern not far from the entrance I could see a broad area of black soil and small chunks of burnt wood. To my surprise I saw a large earthen pot shard lying near the outer fringe of the black ash. The vessel had been broken off about the third of the way down. All that remained was the rim, very thin walled, bearing small indentations. It appeared to be shell tempered. I was certain the cave had not be visited by modern man and if so only briefly and without interest in the early occupants of the shelter.

When I reached the back of the cavern, I discovered yet another room and beyond yet another. I returned to the entrance, removed tools for excavating and although a bit handicapped, set about probing the ash bed to determine if it belonged to modern man or Prehistory Indians. Due to lack of ventilation, dust soon filled the cavern and I was forced to stop the screening and instead paid close attention to the dig. Several limestone's lay near the surface, fie blackened forming a hearth. Many bones were present, representing a wide variety of animals, such as deer, turkey opossum, turtle and a host of others. Many of the larger bones bore cut marks and scrapings in the preparation of cooking or making tools.

After a time I sat sorting through the bones, which had come from the same level, looking for other clues into the lives of the early occupants of the shelter. One particular bone caught my eye, larger than most of them and a deep yellow, measuring one and a quarter inches in length. It appeared polished and rounded and drilled on both ends. I cannot say for certain, but I believe it was a human finger or thumb bone. It was a startling discovery, but not unusual, for like all humans down through time, the Indians were not above displaying parts of their enemy.

I continued digging in the ash deposit area for another hour, locating several potshards, a broken chert drill, two shallow fluted chert points, a hammer stone and chert scraper. Near the outer edge of the ashes about eighteen inches down I discovered the burial of an adult male. The skeleton was not of a young man, for its teeth were worn to the gums or broken off. I did not penetrate any further into the burial and replaced all the material I had excavated.

I took a short coffee break and then began a systematic search around the outer edge of the cavern, locating grinding stones, broken tools and two chert knives that were intact. The two blades were all I took with me. I came at last to the back wall and slowly entered the next cavern, taking the garden spade, small paint brush, flashlight, extra batteries, two candles, magnifying glass and notepad. The cavern gave way to a smaller room with deep pools of clear water along each side, where stalactites and stalagmites stood or hung in various stages of formation and none of them appeared damaged. Near the rear of this room I detected the faint outline of what appeared to be human footprints, but cannot say with absolute certainty, however, small amounts of potshard lay scattered along the wall.

The small cavern gave way to yet another room, very large and a portion of it also contained formations and pools of water and high above I could hear the squeak of bats. About half way through this room the floor became dry and appeared to be a dead-end. A ledge or shelf extended across it, too high up to climb onto and directly below it another much smaller ledge.

Below this second ledge I could see a dark opening where the cave continued on.

Quite weary and not feeling my best I sat down to rest and smoke. During this time I made a final sweep with the light under the ledge. Lying about four feet under the bottom ledge I spotted a stick. Curious I crawled in and retrieved it. The stick was red cedar, heavily charred on the larger end and measured approximately thirty inches in length. A bit puzzle. by the presence of the stick I scooted further under the ledge and laid down on my stomach and moved the light along the back wall to where I had seen the opening. A small low mound caught my eye and I moved further in. There were other bumps and protrusions scattered around and were quickly found to be stones and wood debris. The larger mound appeared suspect and I crawled a few feet and focused the light directly on it. At first it appeared to be an old varmint dig until I saw the top of a skull showing through. Now lying next to it, I began brushing away the dirt and found a small human skull staring at me. The lower jaw lay to one side and bore chew marks. I worked quickly with the brush and spade and soon the skeleton lay completely exposed remarkably intact, down to the tiny finger and toe bones. Some were missing however, scattered a few away in the dirt. The cover of dirt was minimal, only an inch or two, suggesting to me at least it was not an arranged burial.

I was convinced the remains were that of a child, but at that time uncertain what time period the person belonged to. There was no visible modern day clothing of any kind. The skeleton lay in a fetal position, facing me. I gently probed with a finger under the skull and pulled out what appeared to be a dusty spider web and entangled in it I saw a slender cut bone polished and lightly etched. Broad on one end, narrowing to a dull, upturned point, indicating the item was a hair pin and the webbing a tangle of dust encrusted black hair. I looked again at the skeleton to try and determine the sex of the child, but it was so small I was unable to do this with certainty. The remains measured approximately thirty one or thirty eight inches in length. The skull would have fit easily in my hand. The last artifact to be noted was a shell tempered pottery disk about the size of a quarter, drilled though the center. It lay directly in front of the remains and could have been worn around the neck or waste.

I carefully placed dirt over the remains, adding another few inches and with a somber spirit turned away and returned to the front cavern. After packing up the tools, I turned and looked back, quite pleased with all I had found, an ancient shelter appearing not to have been disturbed until my arrival. I stepped back outside into my world, dusty, disfigured somewhat, weary and ready to head home.

I left that cave never to return, piling stones over the entrance, hopefully preserving it for a time. Once again I had traveled into the shadowy world of Prehistory, finding much more than I expected. The secrets of the river still taunting me of life and death, stirring the desire to find more as I continued to explore the ridge and I can only anticipate what else the cave and others have to reluctantly give up to me. They are places that should never be exploited for monetary gain or foolish whims, for after all the underworld where secrets abound belong to no one. Humans are but a small aspect of the Niangua River Legacy, but have changed so much. The story of the little boy or girl I discovered lying in the cave will never be completely revealed, for nature does not give up its secrets easily.

THE END

The Ghost Of Dugan Lane

A narrow dirt road leads away to the south from Highway M, a mile west of Windyville, Missouri. This road is known as Dugan Lane. After leaving the highway, the country road disappears beneath a shroud of trees as it follows the east bank of Indian Creek. Not far down the lane, at the base of a hill once stood a large two story log house. A wide front porch graced the front of the old dwelling and a huge stone fireplace rested against the east end of the Civil War era home. In front of the house stood a small open fronted building and within the gloomy realm a low stone-walled, hand-dug well. Across the road, a little east of the house stood a large barn, constructed of native stone and oak lumber. This property was once the homestead of John and Elizabeth Dugan.

Several years later after the Dugan family moved from the homestead house to a finer home, another family took up residence, a young couple, Emil and Amanda Down, and their infant daughter, Roberta. Amanda a strikingly handsome woman wore her dark shoulder length hair unbound. It is said that she possessed a smile as warm as sunshine and eyes as bright and innocent as a spring day. Truly, they say contented, delighted to be a wife and mother. She enjoyed tending to household chores, working in the garden and above all devoting her life to baby Roberta and husband Emil.

On a particular fateful day in April around the turn of the century, Amanda awakened early as usual, and slipped quietly out of the bed she shared with Emil. Tip-toeing so as not to disturb her husband, she crossed the floor to where Roberta lay sleeping in a crib. Gently she picked up the little girl and crept softly down the narrow stairs to the kitchen. She sat the child down on the floor to play, then began preparing the morning meal. Soon the aroma of biscuits baking and ham frying filled the room. Quite content with the job at hand, Amana bustled about the spacious kitchen.

Roberta meantime enjoyed her freedom exploring the nooks and crannies of the kitchen floor picking up a biscuit crust and eating it. A cricket bent on leaving the house hopped past

Roberta toward the outer door. Laughing, the little girl pursued it, crawling on hands and knees, rising to her feet a time or two. The cricket realizing the danger quickened its pace and with a final leap went out the door onto the porch and disappeared over the edge into the grass below. Roberta intent on catching the insect stood up and toddled to the door.

Preoccupied with her duties, Amanda did not notice her daughter's pursuit of the cricket or that she had left the room. Humming softly to herself, she placed on the table a steaming platter of ham and eggs, a bowl of oatmeal and lastly a covered pan of biscuits.

Still unnoticed by her mother, Roberta with uncertain strides moved out onto the porch and made her way to the stone steps at one end of it. She sat down and eagerly scooted down the three steps to the ground. Plucking a dandelion blossom, popped it into her mouth and then spitting out. She stood up, swaying forward and began walking a wobbly course along the path that led to the well house. A few moments later she dropped to her knees and crawled inside the damp enclosure. The well bucket swaying gently from a pulley overhead caught her attention and unerringly crawled to the stone wall of the well.

Pulling herself up against the stone enclosure with little difficulty and with childish curiosity, Roberta leaned out over the wall peering down into the dark expanse of the well. The shimmering inky blackness of the water demanded her attention and, perhaps reaching out to it leaned further out over the damp slippery wall. Suddenly she lost her hold and toppled headlong into the well.

The baby's cries reverberated piercingly up from the dark deep hole, and then ended abruptly. Nevertheless, the bloodcurdling sound reached Amada. She momentarily stood paralyzed with fear and then ran from the kitchen, nearly tripping on the hem of her night gown. Franticly she called to Roberta, but no answer came. Looking wildly about, screaming she hurried to the steps thinking the little girl had fallen off the porch. She ran toward the well house just as Emil appeared on the porch. Amanda's voice reached a terrible pitch as she ran about searching the yard around her.

Blindly stumbling inside the well house she threw herself to the edge of the murky shaft only to glimpse a tiny hand slipping beneath the shimmering water. Screaming hysterically, completely overwhelmed by the dreadful sight swooned backward and fainted.

They came, many friends and relatives for several days to comfort the grieving couple and to help probed the well for the body of Roberta, but their efforts were futile. Amanda found no comfort and worst of all the body could not be found. One by one the people gave up the attempt. Reduced to a wretched soul, Amanda sat on the front porch weeping, staring at the well house pleading for the return of her beloved daughter. She refused to accept Roberta's death. She rejected all reasoning refusing to give up the hopeless vigil for several days, remaining on the porch still clad in the now soiled white night gown. But as days passed, it seemed she was slowly coming to terms with the tragic loss of Roberta. The dark eyes of Amanda appeared not as haunted, the face less drawn and pale.

In the latter part of June, several weeks following Roberta's drowning, Amanda rose from her bed to a morning fragrant with honeysuckle bloom. Careful not to awaken Emil, she descended the stairs to the kitchen and began preparing the morning meal, humming softly all the while. The young woman's face radiate against the dark sheen of her hair, reminiscent of earlier times. When at last the food was ready she called out sweetly to Emil to come down for breakfast.

Emil, pleased that Amanda had at last accepted the loss of Roberta, hurriedly ate the food for there was much work to be down in the field. Afterward, she followed Emil to the roadside near the barn and lovingly kissed him. She stood by watching as the team of horses was harnessed, waving to him when they started out to the field.

A short time later, Amanda turned as if preoccupied and began walking across the lawn. She stopped short of the porch steps and stood watching Emil and the horses cultivating corn several yards away. A playful breeze tugged mischievously at the hem of the white nightgown and playfully teased the unbound hair. Tears welling up in the sad eyes ran freely down her cheeks. Turning from the steps she began walking toward the well house, slowly at first, quickening the pace and without hesitation entered the small building.

A few moments later the sun rose over a ridge above the house, gently pushing back the last shadows of night. Its light revealed Amanda leaning out over the well weeping brokenly, sobbing mournfully looking down into the darkness of the water. Suddenly she sprang. The gown belled out and her hair streamed upward hiding the tear stained face. Cold water quickly pulled her down into its seemingly illimitable depth, claiming her as it had Roberta.

Once again friends and relatives came and with little difficulty found Amanda's body and a day later it was laid to rest in a church cemetery not far from the homestead. Emil, devastated by a second untimely loss of a loved one, abandoned the farm and in time his tragedies faded in the memories of those left behind. The house remained empty, for no one relished the thought of living there. Amanda's garden soon succumbed to weeds and the house became a drab lonely sight.

One summer night a year or so later after Amanda and Roberta's demise, a man riding a horse along the tree shrouded lane was confronted by the sudden appearance of a tall, fair skinned woman, clothed in a white gown. Long unbound raven hair blowing wildly in the breeze glistened in the moonlight, the face distorted as if in agony. She stood near the center of the road, arms outstretched beseechingly weeping unashamedly. The horse terrified, bolted, throwing the rider. The man scrambled to his feet and though gasping for breath and suffering minor injuries also fled the scene. That man of unquestionable character and honesty never wavered in his account of what he saw one dreadful night along that narrow lane. Until his death years later, he swore that the ghostly image he observed was that of Amanda Down. And it is said the horse who shared the experience could never be ridden again.

Amanda was sighted again several months later, early one morning standing on the porch of the old structure, clad in the gown, an unearthly glow about her face and hair and said to have entered the house climbing the stairs to the loft with a lighted kerosene lamp.

Another sighting of Amanda occurred fifteen years after her death, or so claimed a young woman while walking home one evening. Although frightened, she observed a woman, pale of face with long dark hair clothed in a white gown to her feet, standing near the well house arms outstretched, weeping.

The old barn finally gave way to neglect and fell in a splintered heap of wood and twisted tin. Years later, during the night, the house and well shed mysteriously burned. The remaining rubble was bulldozed over the well.

All that remains of Amanda's world at present is a weed grown meadow and tree shrouded lane. But she is still searching for Roberta, for in the spring of 2005; a motorist reported seeing the figure of a woman dressed in white standing in the morning mist near the site of the homestead house.

THE END

A Tale Of Baldy Mountain

Listen up, for I'm about to take you on a side journey to where men or at least a chosen few were as free as dust devils. Find a stump or mosey bank, settle back and I'll spin the yarn. The place is real, but the people are questionable, ah who knows for certain whether any part of the story is true or not.

They rode off Baldy Mountain and crossed a shadowed lea.

Butcher Redoak, on a mean eyed mule; Twinkles John on a dun with a crooked knee.

Irish Bob sat a pinto, stepping high to the river bank.

Astride their mounts, they sat gazing about, Ozark men ragged and lank.

Irish Bob cradled a Hawkins Rifle; Twinkles John a flintlock Tennessee.

A fifty four smooth bore lay across the Butcher's knee.

Twinkles John spat tobacco, and then nudged the dun.

Irish Bob kicked the pinto and squinted into the sun.

They followed Butcher across the Niangua River and headed up a brushy draw.

Where he reined the mule, pointing to what he saw.

A wisp of smoke drifting high across the trace ahead.

They moved in slow, showing no fear, but horn was ready and round ball lead.

Irish Bob grunted an oath and then gnawed off a chew.

Grinning, John nodded his head, a twinkle a glittering in the Scottish blue eyes.

On the trail stood an old friend, Two Lanterns, wearing buckskins dirty and torn.

They gathered around a smoky fire, Two Lanterns poured coffee into rusty tins.

Two Lanterns divulge a tale, swore it was true of Flat Landers a looking for him.

But he reasoned and reckoned he could handle all seven of them rascals.

Now it wasn't long when they heard the bunch riding hard to where they stood.

The mean eyed mule shied; Butcher shouted and cussed, but it did no good.

He drew a forty four from his belt, took aim and then squeezed off a round.

He peered though the shroud of smoke saw a Flat Lander lying on the ground.

Twinkles John squinted down the barrel of the Tennessee brought a man down laid him to rest.

Irish Bob spat tobacco and the Hawkins roared; a Flat Lander fell ending his quest.

Then Two Lanterns strode to the front of the scene.

He spied a fellow wearing Irish green.

Bringing up his trusted Patriot pistol, he grinned devilishly and held to the left and high.

The dust and smoke settled back and all the Flat Landers were at peace, a laying in the woods.

The mean eyed mule brayed, tossed his head and ran to where Butcher stood.

He whacked the animal across the nose and gave him a boot where it did some good.

They bade two Lanterns a fond farewell, then again crossed the river, up and out across the shadowed lea.

Butcher Redoak on a mean eyed mule; Twinkle John on a dun with a crooked knee.

Irish Bob sat a pinto prancing high up the bank.

Side by side they rode, Ozark men, ragged and lank.

Up Baldy Mountain they went, then turned when they heard a hearty hale.

It was Two Lanterns voice a coming from a brushy vale.

"Ride easy my friends. Keep your powder dry, watch your top knots and be the best you can."

THE END

The Seduction Of Mathew Turner

Sarah Dawson stood at a kitchen window watching her husband Jeb walk slowly down the hill toward the milk barn. Whistling merrily he swung a milk pail in each hand, pushing open the lot gate and then calling to the cows to come. The chore would take at least a couple of hours.

Sarah continued watching Jeb until he entered the barn, anxiously brushing her long brown hair for a second time within an hour. She smoothed out the pink cotton dress she wore over well rounded hips and pulled the low cut garment down a bit further, exposing a little more of her ample breasts. Breathing a sigh of relief when Jeb let in the first two cows, Sarah glanced one last time into the mirror next to the window. Smiling she turned from the mirror, hurried out the front door and ran across the road. Hesitating momentarily she glanced back at the house, then ducked under a barb wire fence and quickly entered a scrub brush thicket at the base of a hill.

Jeb Downing an easy going man, quite friendly and known for his humor was well thought of throughout the county. A stocky built man, no taller than Sarah with a round boyish face and merry blue eyes. Jeb was also an honest man, deeply devoted to the Niangua River bottom farm he had inherited from his parents, but most important he cherished Sarah and trusted her completely. He toiled from sunup to sunset and often quite weary at the end of the day quickly fell a sleep unaware of Sarah stirring restlessly at his side.

Sarah with skirt held high above round plump legs, ran through the ticket, ducking low limbs and upon reaching a huge oak tree stopped. Sweating profusely and out of breath she remained there for a time. Cursing a bit at the wetness on her face and under arms, she pulled the skirt up, wiping the sweat away. Bending over she shook her hair, trying to dry it a bit but soon gave up and looked around the tree up the hill. Smiling, her face flushing, the chestnut eyes sparkling with anticipation at the sight of a man standing on the crest of the hill beneath the drooping boughs of an elm brought forth a new round of sweating. The man was her lover, Mathew Turner. Again she hastily wiped the sweat from her face and arm pits with the hem of the dress and dashed from behind the tree and began running up the hill. Sarah exhibited remarkable grace and agility up the rough rock strewn hill toward Mathew.

Mathew Turner, a confirmed bachelor, part time bartender and field hand considered himself quite the ladies man. He often frequented the town square on Saturday afternoons and randomly attended one of the four churches in the county looking for a lonely woman. It did not matter to him whether they were married or not, young or old as long as they were over twenty one. All women were fair game, the pretty ones the homely, with or without teeth, it just didn't matter to him. Surprisingly, Mathew was not a handsome man, on the contrary quite homely, extremely thin and tall with a hawk nose, thin lips revealing tobacco stained teeth. He wore the same clothes whether tending bar, attending church or working in the field, which consisted of a faded chambray shirt, baggy bib overalls open at the sides and size eleven army surplus boots. He could neither read nor write, but could spout the sweetest poetry that some said attracted women like flies for miles around.

When at last Sarah reached the crest of the hill, she ran to Mathew and he eagerly snatched her to his bosom, stumbling back a bit from the added weight, nevertheless, he began smothering her with kisses, spouting poetry in between the passionate overtures. It was if they were waltzing, although a clumsy one around the tree, but a calculated move by Mathew to a ragged blanket lying on the ground. Moments later in the deep shade of the old tree the lovers spent their passions.

Late one afternoon near chore time a few days after Sarah's rendezvous with Mathew she again waited in the kitchen for Jeb to begin the milking. She stood just inside the door peeking out at her husband sitting on the top porch step leisurely drinking a cup of coffee, the third one in the last hour. The cows were mooing impatiently at the lot gate, yet it appeared Jeb had not taken notice of them.

Glancing at a clock on the wall, Sarah moved out onto the porch and as casually as she could, said. "Jeb it's getting late, aren't you going to milk the cows? I need to know so I can prepare supper."

Jeb did answer and stood up. Sarah ducked back in the kitchen and pretended to be busy about the stove. Smiling mischievously when Sarah heard his footsteps, she began rattling pots and pans expecting to hear the footsteps leaving the porch. But instead of heading to the barn, Jeb strode into the kitchen, set the cup on the table and smiled.

Surprised to say the least, Sarah blurted. "Land a Goshen, Jeb what are you doing? Those cows are hurting and I have no idea when to start supper."

Still smiling, quite pleasantly at that, Jeb gently took her by the arm and led her from the kitchen into the bedroom. Sarah followed obediently, blushing at the thought of what was about to happen.

Jeb spoke very gently when reaching the bed. "Remove your dress Sarah and lay down on the bed. The cows can wait, there's more pressing business to take care of and then you can start supper."

Smiling in anticipation, Sarah removed the light green summer dress and lay down without further word. She smoothed her long tresses across the pillow and watched as Jeb removed from a hip pocket of his overalls a length of rope.

"What on earth are you going to do with the rope?' she asked, a bit puzzled.

"Tie you up my dear," he replied.

More startled then afraid, Sarah tried to sit up but was gently pushed back. Jeb climbed up on the bed a straddle of his wife. Squirming a bit under the two hundred pound man, she tied to wiggle out from under him, but in vain.

"Jeb Dawson you get off me this instant!" she cried angrily. "Have you lost your mind? Why are you doing this to me?"

"I love you Sarah," was all he would say and bound her hands to the headboard.

Kicking screaming, Sarah cried, tears steaming down her cheeks. "You don't love me or you wouldn't do this. Please let me go, please!"

Grimacing now, Jeb slid off the bed, grasped Sarah's feet and tied them to the bed posts. He then slipped out of his overalls, picked up Sarah's dress and held it up. He placed it over his head and began pulling it down, tugging it in place. A bit too tight in the hips, but it hung about him nevertheless. Smiling again, even broader, mirth bright in the blue eyes he turned to the dresser and opened the top drawer. From it he removed a green shawl and wrapped it around his head. He looked in the mirror, the eyes bright and merry. Stepping to the side of the bed, he gently fluffed the pillow under Sarah's head, bowed and then quickly left the room.

Sarah, upon realizing what Jeb was about to undertake, moaned, turned her face shamefully into the pillow closing her eyes, weeping softly.

Mathew Turner pacing around the elm tree grew noticeably more irritated by the moment. Sarah was late and he began wondering if she would come at all. He had once scolded her for being tardy and reckoned he would have to listen again to her plaintive excuses. To keep her in line, an especially severe scolding was needed. He smiled. Sarah was like putty in his hands particularly when he spouted poetry and all though he would not admit it, the woman was his favorite.

He saw her then darting from the thicket, running up the hill toward him. Burning with anticipation, Mathew began waving, smiling broadly.

Jeb had stood for a time in the brush, closely observing Mathew pacing about the tree. A devilish smirk played across his face and the eyes glistened with dark humor. Pulling the dress further down over his legs, taking a deep breath, he darted from the brush into the clearing.

Mathew, beside himself with desire continued waving, hopping up and down gleefully. Sarah appeared especially plump running up the hill and he marveled at the agility of the woman. Never before had he been so taken with a woman and decided to ask her to run away with him. There was an abandoned shack or two on Greasy Creek. They could take up residence in one of them and she would be at his beck and call any time he desired.

Jeb in the meantime ran up the rocky slope, closing the gap between him and Mathew. Waving, squealing, he never broke stride and soon arrived on the crest of the hill and stopped a short distance from the tall man he despised.

Mathew, unaware of the deception about to take place did not wait for his lover to come to him, but instead sprinted forward with outstretched arms. Unsuspecting of the shrouded face he rushed in and pulled Jeb into his arms and puckered up.

It of course was not the eager lips of Sarah that met his, but a steel hard fist. Mathew reeled backward stunned by the impact and barely regained his footing when he received another resounding blow to the side of his head and staring in disbelief into the eyes peering out from under the shawl.

Squalling, pleading for mercy Mathew fell to his hands and knees and began running like a whipped dog on all fours. He made it to the timber line, stood up and saw Jeb Dawson leaning against the tree waving timidly, blowing kisses.

THE END

Author's woodcarving of an 1880's lawman

Rendezvous At Buffalo Head

No one knows for certain exactly what started the ruckus at the Dog Leg Saloon sometime around midnight, September 8, 1892 and erupted into a fracas ending with one bar girl dead as well as the owner of the infamous saloon and the building in flaming ruins.

The Dog Leg Saloon, constructed of cedar logs, sat perched high on Scott Bluff overlooking the Niangua River. It began tame enough three years earlier, a quite place for the local men to slip off from home to drink and carouse with the bar girls. Chester R. Reynolds or Judge Reynolds as most folks called him inherited the land from his father.

Judge Reynolds a rather tall stout man with shaggy sandy hair and a mess of freckles had dabbled in preaching until run out of a county in north Missouri. He took to free lance judging, but after sentencing a man to hang found himself on the run from the Feds. He made his way to the boot heel of Missouri and was taken in by a black Baptist minister. Judge Reynolds married the minister's only daughter and appeared to settle down. A couple of years later the wife caught him cavorting with a local white girl and she too ran him off after shooting him in the left foot with a four ten shotgun. And so it came to be a year later in the spring of 1889, the Dog Leg Saloon rose above the river, named after the owner whose twisted left foot and leg resembled the hind leg of a dog.

Sitting quietly on their mounts a group of Ridge Runners, or so they called themselves, waited in a thicket of sumac for the Dog Leg to open at the appointed hour of Five p.m. Long evening shadows obscured the riders and above them restless clouds moved northward, tinged red by the sunset. Other riders began to appear from the dark wall of the forest, making their way to the saloon.

When at last lantern light appeared in the windows of the saloon and the front door swung open, fifteen Ridge Runners moved out from their concealment and began the short ride to the establishment. They hurried not, keeping a wary eye open for the presence of a law man. Bristling with an assortment of long rifles and a few new fangled cartridge revolvers the bunch rode in silence behind their unspoken leader, Two Lanterns.

Two Lanterns riding a high stepping bay mare listened to the talk around him. Most of the men were discussing what would happen when they returned to camp after a night in the Dog Leg.

"That woman of mine ain't gonna treat me kindly when she finds out about me taking the last three dollars we have and spending it on liquor," said one man riding a raw bone mule."

"Well I'll tell you what I'm gonna do," said another. "I'll whup the day lights out of my woman and then go to bed."

Two Lanterns laughed. "Sure you will just like the last time when she knocked your front teeth out with a stick of stove wood. I'm tired of listening to you all whining. So just shut your mouths before I shut them."

Two Lanterns a born and bred Tennessean, reared by an Irish immigrant father and Cherokee mother did not take well to the laws of the land. A small bone man, barely five foot eight, dark complexioned with piercing black eyes, harbored a temper easily roused and could turn deadly at the least provocation. Unkempt gray black hair hung to his shoulders, tied back with a dirty bandanna and an equally bedraggled mustache covered his mouth. A friend to few for he considered friendship a sacred thing. Armed only with a long barrel single shot smooth bore pistol known as the "Kentucky Patriot," with a trigger pull near zero, Two Lanterns lead the misfits on across the field to the Dog Leg Saloon.

Many others were also converging on the saloon, mostly farmers, some were church going gents bent on a few hours of drinking to lessen the burden of their drab existence. Behind them, near the edge of the timber a little east of the saloon sat a man on a black gelding, watching the possession of men. A wide brim hat shadowed the thin face, but the waning light of the sun revealed blue eyes and cigarette dangling from tightly drawn lips. Red hair hung to the man's shoulders with a mustache of the same hue obscuring the mouth somewhat. Most people knew him simply as Ira, Ira Ikerred a former scout with the Missouri Militia. Ira alone bore the stigma of killing Lone Eagle when the Indian refused to take his followers to Oklahoma and embittered with the deed, blamed Captain Butcher Redoak for ordering him to assassinate the man. Upon learning that Butcher had left the militia and became a state marshal, Ira decided to find the man and settle the score.

Night fell around the Dog Leg and inside could be heard the woeful sound of a fiddle and the stomping of feet. The place was packed with at least seventy people, including Judge Reynolds and a half a dozen bar girl. "The Rivers Queens," as the Judge liked to call them were quite well known up and down the river as far away as Baldy Mountain and Barefoot Pass. Rose Marie the boss lady oversaw Crystal Clear, Shanda Lyre, Ima Mazing, Rockie Bell and Tingaling Star wasted no time relieving the men of their money by whatever means it took, all except Rose Marie who could not stomach the foul odors emitting from most of the patrons.

Cursing, yodeling, dancing, the drunken crowd grew more boisterous as the evening progressed. Two Lanterns and Twinkles John sat at a corner table drinking whiskey, laughing and talking and appearing to have a good time.

"Ain't this something, kind of like the good old days in the Colorado Mountains," said Twinkles.

"Yeah I reckon," answered Two Lanterns, except for them dirt farmers that keep piling in here. There was a time when Flat Landers like them would have been run off or shot where they stood. "I'll tell you something else that grieves me and that is Butcher Redoak turning lawman. He rode with us Twinkles, slept and ate with us and a dang good mountain man, or so I thought."

"Awe Two Lanterns, times change, people change. Besides he ain't doing you no harm." said Twinkles John. "And as for the farmers, they're just trying to have a good time, making it the best way they can."

"I reckon," replied Two Lanterns, but Butcher is another story and I aim to ask him why he turned the way he did. I trusted that man and considered him a friend."

"Heck he still is as long as you don't go and break the law."

"He ain't no friend of mine," declared Two Lanterns. "I hear he's got that forty four of his full of notches, killing men that wouldn't obey his law."

"If what you say is the truth, he killed them because they were gunning for him," said Twinkles. "I never knew of him shooting an unarmed man or anyone in the back."

"No I reckon not, but I hear that feller who rode with him in the militia is gunning for him. It seems the man is madder than a wet hen over Butcher ordering him to kill that Osage Chief in an ambush. Butcher is gonna have to face the feller someday."

"Well it ain't none of my business," Twinkles replied, "and I don't think it's any of yours either."

"I tell you one thing you half breed Scotsman, nobody tells me what my business is!" retorted Two Lanterns. "You keep talking that way and I'll give you a taste of the Patriot."

"Awe quit your braying," Twinkles replied. ""'I'm about as afraid of you as I am a chigger crawling up my leg. Drink up friend this ain't no time to be getting all riled up."

Cursing, jumping to his feet, Two Lanterns brought up the Patriot. The sudden movement set off the gun, smashing an overhead lantern a few feet away. Hot glass and burning kerosene rained down on unsuspecting men standing at the bar. Old Man Satterfield took a shard of glass in his right eye and fell screaming to the floor. An angry howl went up across the smoke filled room. Two men at the door, who had been arguing brandishing their revolvers, shot two more lanterns from the rafters. The fire spread quickly after that.

Standing in another corner of the saloon, Ira quietly observed the impending storm of anger and fear that now rage across the floor. He expected at any moment to see Marshal Redoak enter and bring order to the saloon, instead saw black smoke billowing up from the sawdust covered floor and men falling on one another.

Judge Reynolds leaped on the bar and began shouting. "You dang fools put the fire out, before it gets out of control you idiots! If the place burns I ain't gonna build back and you all will just have to stay home with your women."

Three shots rang out, two of them hitting the Judge between the eyes and the other one, a wild shot hitting Tingaling

Star in the back killing her instantly. The entire melee lasted only a couple of minutes.

"Two Lanterns look what you've caused!" Twinkles John yelled, snatching up his hat.

Laughing, Two Lanterns replied. "I couldn't have done better if I planned it. Judge Reynolds got what he deserved. I can't say that about the poor darling girl. Come on let's get out of here! There's gonna be one heck of a fire shortly."

"There's going to be more than that to pay when the Marshal hears about this," Twinkles John said.

Like rats leaving a sinking ship, so were the troupe of men Two Lanterns had brought to the now doomed Dog Leg Saloon. They gathered outside away from danger, cursing and hollering drinking whiskey snatched from the bar. Pure pandemonium along with the fire spread though the building, forcing several men up against the south wall. Rose Marie succeeded in gathering all of her girls around her, except for the unfortunate Tingaling Star who lay beneath burning debris. Smoke swirled about them, forcing the women to the floor. Moments later they reached a secret trap door that led beneath the building and freedom to a brushy area out back. Coughing, stumbling through the brush, the women turned westward toward Buffalo Head, some eighteen miles away.

One man cowering with six farmers at the south wall pulled from a pocket of his overalls a stick of dynamite and shoved it behind a stud. Their only hope was to blow a hole in the wall and escape through it. Few if any of the other men lying on the floor around them noticed the dynamite. A lighted cigar was pressed to the short fuse and the six men took cover beneath the burning bar. Seconds later the stick of dynamite exploded blowing out most of the wall, sending it spiraling down some fifty feet into the river. Seventeen men and a large Red Bone hound fell to their death on the rocky bank below. The six farmers and several other men rushed out into the cool night air. The building swayed cracking and groaning and fell over the bluff in a splintered burning heap. The death toll, although it was not known for certain was said to have been fifteen men and one woman.

Ira ran from the building early on to his horse standing tied in a grove of walnut trees a few yards from the saloon. He sat there for a few moments rolling a cigarette, grim of face listen to the screams of the people inside. Nudging the black gently with his spurs, he turned westward toward Buffalo Head.

Buffalo Head, situated on the south end of Fifteen Mile Prairie sat on a low hill around a town square where in the center stood a court house. The Laclede Hotel one of many businesses around the square including a theater, stage depot, jail and livery stable made up the small prairie town. A drab, dusty place at best, but welcomed by the many people who came to town to shop, lay over on their way west or hang out at the Rusty Bucket Saloon. The saloon set on the southern outskirts of the town. East of the square Graveyard Road meandered past a dozen of more homes across the road from a rather huge cemetery. At the end of the road lay a field littered with wagons in need of repair along with discarded furniture and the skeletal remains of horses, cattle and hogs, abandoned by travelers seeking homestead land. The unsightly field also catered to drifters and other riffraff and most townspeople did not go there for fear of being robbed or worse. The only two buildings standing on the property were two privies, havens for wasps, lizards, tumble bugs and occasional Copper Head snake.

Marshal Butcher Redoak stood on the porch of the old Prairie Theater, next to his deputy, Gentleman George Hilderbrand. The deputy cradled in one arm a double barrel, twelve gage Greener shotgun. The Marshal watched intently a group of at least forty rag tag people riding past the theater heading down Graveyard Road. He lit a cigarette and then shook his head in disgust.

"Looks like the old campground will be full tonight," Mused the Gentleman. "Are going to leave them alone like we do other drifters that take up residence down there?"

"No we have to pay a visit to let them know there is law in town," the Marshal replied. "I hope they are just passing through. I don't like the smell of the bunch. That little feller riding the skinny bay looks familiar and if he's who I think he is, there's bound to be trouble."

"Who might he be?"

"Two Lanterns, a man I once rode with over on Baldy mountain several years ago when beaver hides were worth trapping. He didn't then and still doesn't have any use for lawmen. I guess he has a reason, but I never heard what it was. He can be a mean feller and even though we parted friends, I doubt if he feels that way now."

"Is that the bunch suspected of at least helping to burn down the Dog Leg Saloon a night or two ago?" asked the deputy.

"Yeah it sure is," answered the Marshal. "There was nothing left when I got there the day after the incident. Several charred bones and smoking ash lay where the saloon had stood. Most of the building fell over the bluff. The best tally I came up with was fifteen dead men and one woman. The woman was a daughter of old man Tucker Jones, former owner and originator of the Rusty Bucket. That gal sure made a mess of her life, but I doubt if Tucker gives a hoot."

"Good lord, Tucker must be close to a hundred years old," the deputy replied. "I hear tell he had kids by several women and never took care of even one of them. The gal was one of Rose Marie's girls wasn't she?"

"Yeah they came into Buffalo Head night for last about done in," the Marshal said. "I hear they went to work in the Rusty Bucket."

"Yeah I heard that to," replied the deputy. "Rose Marie never did strike me as a bar girl and least of all a madam. Never could figure out why she does what she does."

"Oh I suppose after she lost her husband in that stage coach roll over on the Fort Scott Road, hard times drove her into the saloons. Except for the dishonest way she takes money from men, I never knew of her selling it. She's an avid opera fan and attends the theater quite often, and is forced to set alone in one of the boxes on the second level."

The two men continued their conversation, delaying their visit to the camp ground. Marshal Redoak a tall blue eyed redhead man of forty odd years, who's scarred leather vest covered a blue cotton shirt and dark britches. On his right hip he wore a holstered, ivory handled Colt, forty four. Twenty six notches cut deep in the handle of the revolver; a grim reminder of the men who had faced him and died. A nickel plated, Missouri State Marshal's badge sagged from the vest.

Gentleman George Hilderbrand, also tall but with dark restless eyes, black curly hair and finely molded face wore his Spanish heritage proudly, often defiantly. Ten years younger than Butcher and unwise in many aspects of law men's work often took chances the Marshal frowned on. Born of a German father and Mexican mother the Gentleman acquired his height from the German blood and the passion from Mexican rich tradition of leaping before thinking. Trimly clothed in a white embroidered shirt, black leather britches and knee high boots cast him as an outstanding figure of a man.

"Marshal, why did you cut those notches in the handle of your Colt, surely you don't have to reminded of the men you've killed?" the Gentleman asked.

Smiling faintly, the Marshal answered a bit gruffly. "No I don't have to be reminded. The Lord knows I've killed too many men. I thought maybe if I cut those notches it might discourage some hot head of a young man from drawing on me."

"Has it?"

"Yes," the Marshal replied. "Sammy Ingalls confronted me one night in front of the Rusty Bucket about a year ago. He called me an old has been and a few other choice names and then informed me he was going to shoot me. Well I managed to steer him under a street light and he took one look at these notches and fled the scene. There have been others who changed their minds at the last minute. I will say this; most of the men I killed deserved it."

"Sammy wanted to shoot you?" laughed the Gentleman. "Why heck he's married now with twin daughters and fixing to turn preacher."

"My point exactly, smiled the Marshal. "Let's get the horses and pay a visit to those people setting up camp."

Lester Youngblood, a small weathered man of undetermined years and breed sat astride a rangy buckskin stallion supervising the setting up of the dozen or more camps north of the main grounds that was relatively free of rubbish. He held in one hand a flint lock rifle, waving and shouting to a couple of men who were about to square off with their rifles. "Remember this brothers, which ever one of you is left standing is gonna be shot in the head. Get back to work and help your women set up the camps."

Lester dismounted and motioned to a group of Buck Skinners squatted around a jug of moonshine, threatening them with bodily harm if they didn't get busy. Although they were noticeably defiant shaking their fists and such, they didn't ague and scattered to different areas of the camp. A lean and rowdy bunch that understood Lester when he waved the flint lock, for to ignore him meant certain death. Most of the eighteen men in the group kept at least one woman and a few of them two or more. The half dozen children were a motley lot; most were naked, howling and fighting like wolf cubs.

A hodgepodge of lodges soon stood in the high weeds, teepees, Baker tents along with a couple of covered wagons. In the center of the camp a hedge fire burned, crackling loudly. A huge cast iron kettle was set up over the fire and an assortment of ingredients tossed in. Carrots, beets, potatoes and several large onions disappeared into the murky water. A cry went up at one of the privies and a young boy ran toward the camp holding up two large opossums. Yanked from his hands they were quickly slain, gutted, skinned and thrown in the kettle amidst a rousing cheer. The largest of the children, a girl, snatched up the opossum skins and ran into a Bakers tent.

Two Lanterns sat alone on a buffalo hide, smoking a cigar. He kept a close eye on his possessions which wasn't much, a pistol, powder horn, a tin of caps, tin cup, plate and assorted clothing. Smaller than most of the men in camp, but as fierce as a badger and had been known to whip three men in a fight, kicking, gouging and biting to win.

A clatter of hooves on the road leading into the camp sent Lester running to the stallion. He quickly mounted the horse, pulled the hammer back on the rifle, grimaced and turned to face the sound and waited.

A moment or so later, Marshal Redoak and the Gentleman appeared. Dropping the hammer on the flint lock, Lester raised a hand and waved. "Hello gents, welcome to the Ozark Ridge Runners camp."

"Are you the leader?" asked the Marshal.

"Can't say I am, but people listen to me," replied Lester.

"How long you all figuring on staying here?" the Marshal asked, eying Lester closely.

Lester's eyes narrowed a bit before answering. "Oh I don't know, maybe a couple of days, could be longer. Why, any problem with that?"

The gentleman laughed, swinging the Greener to bear on Lester's head.

Marshal Redoak frowned, motioned for him to bring up the shotgun. "No I don't have a problem with you people staying here a few days as long as you don't clean out the hen houses or come into town looking for trouble. I want you to stay out of the Rusty Bucket. I don't want it to burn like the Dog Leg did. You got any hot heads in camp?"

Lester appeared to ponder the question, picking at a wart on his chin. "Well, I suppose you could say every one of us including the women don't like being pushed around or cussed at, but that feller over there beats all of us." he answered, pointing to Two Lanterns.

"He looks familiar, what's his name?" asked the Marshal.

"He goes by Two Lanterns," Lester replied. "He don't like law men or farmers."

Grinning, Marshal Redoak focused on Two Lanterns still sitting on the Buffalo hide. "I've heard that," he replied. "He was always a bit touchy about the law."

"You know him then?"

"Yeah afraid I do," answered the Marshal. "I wintered with him on Baldy Mountain. We probably trapped the last of the beaver in the Niangua River. He's still got that old moth eaten Buffalo Hide. I've seen him wrap up in that thing below zero a lying on the frozen ground as snug as a bug in a rug. "I'll go over and say hello."

Marshal, I wouldn't do that if I were you," said Lester.

"Well that's my business," replied the Marshal. "Why does he dislike lawmen?"

"Well I've heard it said a gal he was favoring was thrown into jail in Corkrey for prostitution. She claimed she was innocent, but they locked her up anyway. She hung herself during the night. Two Lanterns ain't ever got over that, so my advice to you is to leave him alone. I can't say I blame him for feeling the way he does."

"I'm not walking away," answered Marshal Redoak. "He's an old friend and I'm not gonna turn tale because he's got something stuck in his craw. Come on deputy I reckon this won't take long."

Two Lanterns, upon seeing Marshal Redoak and Gentleman George making their way toward him, picked up the Kentucky Patriot and brought the hammer back to full cock. He carefully laid it across one knee and waited.

"Howdy Two Lanterns, it's been awhile," said the Marshal, eying the pistol.

"It ain't been long enough," Two Lanterns replied looking up. "You're not welcome in my camp, so I would advice you to take that Mexican and get out of here. You got about thirty seconds before I blow your head off."

"You do that and the Mexican as you call him will splatter you all over this hill side and half the prairie." The Marshal said regarding the man intently.

Two Lanterns shrugged, but kept his hands where they lay. "So it be," he said. "A man's camp is hollowed ground. Have you forgotten?"

"No I haven't," answered the Marshal, "but it grieves me you feel the way you do."

"Then take off that filthy badge and toss it into the fire."

"I can't do that,"

"Then leave," Two Lanterns said, placing his right hand on the butt of the Patriot, "or I'll kill you where you stand."

Gentleman George brought up the Greener and in the same motion pulled both hammers back. "I'll take you out before you can bring up that monstrosity you call a pistol," he growled.

"No you wouldn't," the Marshal replied. "The man can strike like a snake. I would be dead before you could pull a trigger. We'll leave, Two Lanterns. I have no grievance against you and I'm sorry you feel the way you do, but from this moment on we are strangers and if you come into town for any reason I'll arrest you or kill you, which ever comes first."

"That sounds fair enough to me," Two Lanterns said. "As far as I'm concerned you ain't any better than a tick infested cur dog or a dirt farmer."

Two Lanterns sat for a time staring up the road Marshal Redoak and the Gentleman had departed. Laying the Patriot aside he reached for the rusty cup, stood up and made his way to the center of the camp where sat a jug of moonshine whiskey. He filled the cup to the brim, drank it down in one breath, then filled it again and returned to his spot. The dark eyes of the man again took up vigilance on the Graveyard Road.

Evening shadows slowly made their way up the slope into the Ozark Ridge Runners camp, crossing the Buffalo Hide where Two Lanterns sat. A short time later the sun slipped below the horizon, freeing the shadows to travel at will. Two Lanterns with the Patriot in hand stood up, kicked dirt over his fire and without a word to the others strode onto the Graveyard road and began walking toward the town square.

Word came to Butcher and the Gentleman that a Buck Skinner seen on the Graveyard Road had boasted he was gunning for the Marshal and the Mexican deputy. Neither of the men appeared surprised at the news and leisurely finished their coffee before stepping out onto the street. Lantern light glowed from the front entrance of the Prairie Theater where several people had gathered waiting to attend a show soon to take place inside. A troupe of actors stood in the ally smoking and laughing. Across the street from the theater the dusky light winked eerily from the stain glass window of the Buffalo Head Baptist church. Shadows lurked on each side of the building waiting for darkness to settle upon the town.

"Let's take a look around the theater first," Butcher said, loosening the Colt in its holster. "Keep a sharp eye George; he could be anywhere or nowhere. Have you got the hammers back on the Greener?"

"Yeah I do," replied the Gentleman.

"Then keep the dang thing pointed up," the Marshal said. "I don't want an innocent bystander cut down."

"There are a lot of people out tonight," the Gentleman said. "I reckon that melodrama playing in the theater brought them out for a night of play acting."

"Yeah I suppose," answered Marshal Redoak. "No more talk Deputy, concentrate on what you see and don't see' your life depends on it. If Two Lanterns is out here bent of killing us, I guarantee he won't give us much of a warning and maybe none."

A few moments later the pair came to a blacksmith shop adjacent to the theater and in the dimly lit entrance stood Rose Marie. The small redhead woman's face appeared especially pale against the light of the lantern hanging above her. She smiled and lifted a dainty hand in greeting.

"Good evening Rose," the Marshal said quietly. "Are you attending the show in the theater this evening?"

Smiling she stepped from the doorway, looking up into Butcher's face, the blue eyes appearing a bit fearful. "Yes, I hear it is a delightful comedy," she answered. "But as I stood waiting for the doors to open I began wishing I hadn't come. I hear that awful man called Two Lanterns is on the prowl. You and your deputy should be cautious, for he is a very dangerous man."

"Rose Marie, don't be concerned about him, go and enjoy the show," the Marshal replied. "If he is out here looking for trouble, we'll take care of it."

Shaking her head doubtfully, Rose said. "I'm not so sure you can Marshal. Any one of those shadows along the street could be hiding the man. Please be careful. I'm leaving Buffalo Head on the noon stage tomorrow. I'm going back to Springfield, Missouri the place of my birth and try to start over. Perhaps you should consider another line of work."

Looking down into the face of the woman, he found something there that held him for a few seconds in silence; perhaps a reflection of his own loneliness. "I hope you find a better life," was all he could think of to say.

The lawmen parted company when they reached the theater, with Butcher crossing the street to the church. The darkness closed in as he made his way past the building. The hair on the back of his neck seemed to stand on end, knotting his stomach, tightening the hand resting on the butt of the Colt. Each step brought a deepening sense of uneasiness, tightening the corners of his mouth, certain that danger was imminent. .

"Butcher Redoak," a voice hailed from somewhere in the shadows behind him. "I never thought I'd see the day you'd be wearing a lawman's badge. Take it off or die!"

Frowning, the Marshal hastened forward toward the sound of the voice he recognized as that of Two Lanterns. "Like I told you before, I've got a job to do and it ain't none of your business. I'll give you one last chance, get out of town."

Two Lanterns stepped out onto the walk way, a ragged figure with shinning eyes. Shaking his head sadly, the Marshal drew the Colt. Quicker than the blink of an eye, Two Lanterns vanished into the cloak of darkness, laughing taunting the Marshal. Crouching low, the lawman ran along side the church building expecting the man to stand and fight. But as he reached the rear corner of the building, the loud click of a hammer being drawn back sent chills down his spine. He turned to glimpse Two Lanterns sighting down the barrel of the Kentucky Patriot. The Marshal stumbled, fell face down, shot in the head.

The roar of Two Lanterns smooth bore sent the Gentleman running across the street. He quickly found the Marshal lying in a clump of tall grass. Many of the town's people rushed from the buildings along the street to where the Marshal lay, to see him dead or watch him die. But to their surprise they found the lawmen sitting up.

"Go on about your business," the Gentleman ordered, "He ain't dead and only grazed by the shot. That Buckskinner should have aimed a bit more to the left and high. Now get!"

Not far away, up the street from the church in an alley, stood Ira smoking a cigarette, weary and dusty but smiling at the words of the Gentleman. "Ah Butcher," he said, "You will face me now Captain."

Two Lanterns also heard the words of the Gentleman and like a coyote slipped away into the night. He stealthy entered the camp at the end of Graveyard road, picked up his possessions, nodded to Lester and headed up a ridge to spend the night, for he knew Butcher Redoak would come looking for him.

Three days later a prairie breeze cooled the August morning and as most folks awakened they wondered if the Marshal was up and on his way to track down Two Lanterns. Word of the shooting had spread far and wide and many had come to Buffalo Head to see if Marshal Redoak and Gentleman George would settle the score. There was Twinkles John, Irish Bob and Banjo Boats to name a few. They too had rode with the Marshal across Barefoot Pass to the Baldy Mountain Lair. No one had come to town to take sides, but see which man would end the fracas. There were those who had shared a fire with two Lanterns, drying their skins on a cold winter night. A theater troupe singing folk songs set up on the square and put on a show, and a fiddler who played Shenandoah and the prettiest waltz you ever heard. The Cherokee came to sit and wait.

Marshal Redoak rose early that day, feeling fit enough to begin the hunt for Two Lanterns. He did not care whether he brought the man back dead or alive. A deep red gash lay over the Marshal's right eye and he squinted as he stepped out onto the town square. Gentleman George stood waiting, cradling the Greener in one arm.

"Good lord deputy where'd all these people come from," asked the Marshal.

The Gentleman laughed. "I expect some came from miles around," said he. "Are you up for breakfast?"

"I sure am," the Marshal answered. "I've a slight headache, but a shot of whiskey later will ease it."

"Have you considered where Two Lanterns might be?" The Gentleman asked.

Glancing down the street, Marshal Redoak quickly scrutinized a group of people standing around a display of handmade chairs, bed frames and axe handles. Further down the street a display of quilts had attracted several people. "The town has turned into a carnival," he replied. "To answer your question about where Two Lanterns might be hiding, I know where he is." He's not gonna give up and what better place to be than right here in Buffalo Head. I don't know exactly where he is, but he could be hiding out in the Ridge Runners camp or in one of the many upstairs rooms along the street. Then again he may be squatted down behind a privy. It doesn't matter, because he's gonna show himself, probably today."

Turning to face the street, Gentleman George glanced about. "Do you think he will try to sneak up on you?"

"No not this time," replied the Marshal. "He'll be sober and walk out on the street to face me." What worries me is that some of those Ridge Runners may be with him. I don't want any of the town's people hurt, so it best to keep a sharp eye out for them drifting into town."

"Good lord Marshal! Do you think we can handle them?"

"Yeah I do," he replied. "How many shells you got in that fancy bandoleer?"

"Twenty two rounds with sixty grains of powder." The gentleman answered. "Do you think that's enough?"

"A plenty if you don't die first. I hope they are they all double 0 loads?"

"Yes the Gentleman answered, fingering the shells.

"Let's get some breakfast and a couple of good cigars."

Ira stepped slowly out of the main door of the Laclede Hotel, watching the Marshal and deputy walking along the street toward the Bison Inn. Clean shaven and wearing a riding coat, he waited until the pair had disappeared inside the café and then made his way to the livery stable, where he saddled the black gelding and lead him outside to a hitching rail and tied him. From there he walked to a bench under an elm tree on the court house lawn, sat down and rolled a cigarette. Obscured somewhat beneath the deep shade, he settled back to wait.

Rose Marie sat in a corner booth facing the door of the Bison Inn and immediately observed the Marshal and Gentleman George enter the café. Next to her on the floor sat a large carpet bag. Clothed in a dark skirt and white ruffled blouse, the red head could easily been have been mistaken for a schoolmarm, but she sat alone and no one appeared to give her a second look.

"Marshal Redoak," she called out softly, "I'm glad to see you on your feet. At first I heard that you had been killed, but then later learned you suffered only a slight wound."

"Rose Marie!" The Marshal exclaimed. "I figured you were in Springfield by now."

"I'm leaving on the noon stage," she replied. "I was hoping you would be on that stage and leave this town behind, but of course I see you're still wearing the badge."

"I can't leave now," he said, "maybe another day."

"I'm sorry," she replied looking up. "The future has a way of saying no."

"It's good to see you again Rose," the Marshal answered, avoiding the melancholy he saw in the blue eyes."

Sometime later, the lawmen strode out of the Bison Inn, each smoking a cigar. Gentleman George walked to the left of Redoak, the Greener at half cock cradled in one arm. People were scurrying from the street to the alleys and a woman nearby hushed her baby's cry and then ran from the street. Two Lanterns stood in the middle of the street, about twenty yards away, waving the Patriot high over his head.

Side stepping off the walk way to the center of the street, Marshal Redoak said quietly to Gentleman George. "Look up to your left deputy in that window over the hardware store, one of the Ridge Runners."

The Greener roared blowing out the glass, sending the man careening backwards to his death. The Marshal drew the Colt, firing it once into an alley on his right and a Ridge Runner staggered forth and dropped to the walkway. Again the Greener spit fire, cutting a man down. A Hawkins Rifle let loose with round ball lead hitting Gentleman George deep in the chest. Mortally wounded he fell to his knees bringing up the Greener sending the man with the Hawkins to his death and then fell dead face down.

Only two men stood now in the shroud of smoke, Marshal Butcher Redoak and Two Lanterns, once friends from the Baldy Mountain Lair.

"You're not walking away from this Two Lanterns," the Marshal shouted.

Cursing, Two Lanterns brought up the Patriot, one shot to find the Marshal and take him out. The Marshal's Colt roared, once then twice, driving hot lead into the body of the Ridge

Runner. The Patriot sagging a bit spewed fire and its load of double 0 buckshot into the dust a few yards from where the Marshal stood. Dropping the Patriot, Two Lanterns turned and began walking away, only to stumble and fall dead at the front steps of the Church.

It is likely the two passengers on board the noon stage in Buffalo Head, for all appearances found the town quite peaceful. Not many people were on the street as it pulled up in front of the depot. In fact only three people were visible. Rose Marie stood waiting under a canopy, the paleness of her face in stark contrast to the white blouse she wore. Two men stood further on down the street facing each other. Marshal Redoak, his face drawn and tight lipped, stood facing Ira Ikerred.

"Marshal, You ruined my life the day you ordered me to kill Lone Eagle," Ira said. "You had no business doing that. He should have been given the chance to defend himself like I'm giving you now."

"I'm sorry you feel that way Ira," replied the Marshal.

Only one shot rang out a second or two later and Marshal Redoak lay dead on the town square of Buffalo Head.

THE END

Christmas, the queen of her domain

The Journey

Dedicated To The Memory of Christmas

The feral cat cautiously moved stealthily from a thicket of buck brush to the edge of a deeply rutted muddy road. The large female although very thin proceeded with the self assurance of a predator. Covered with long white unkempt fur, she paused crouching motionless, staring straight ahead at a sparrow fluttering noisily in the center of the road. The sparrow turned and began pecking in the mud and once again the cat crept forward, her tail twitching ever so slightly. Appearing as little more than a gray shadow sliding across the road in the afternoon sun, the cat drew to within striking distance of the bird.

A few feet behind the female, a wet calico kitten tumbled from the buck brush and clawed its way up the shallow ditch to the road side and stopped, followed by a second kitten, appearing black in color. They began mewing in unison, alerting the sparrow to danger. Pouncing, the female sprung in a desperate attempt to bring down the prey, but too late, the bird flew up into the trees overhead.

The distraction of the kittens and losing the bird failed to alert the large cat to the steady drone of a truck engine approaching a sharp curve to the east of the trio. The female quickly ran to the kittens and laid down for them to suckle, silencing the whimpering. Suddenly a large cattle truck sped around the curve, providing little time for the unfortunate three to run away to safety. The female squalled, jumped to her feet, snatched up one of the kittens and attempted flee to the roadside. The second kitten followed close behind her, but the perilous flight ended abruptly under the tires of the truck. All three lay crushed to death in a pool of muddy water. A dreadful silence prevailed as the sound of the truck faded into the distance.

The late afternoon sunlight slowly faded and the air became noticeably cooler. The mud and patches of dirty snow slush began freezing. A thin veil of clouds moved across the waning sun, darkening the sky. From deep within the brush came the cry of another kitten and the sound of clawing as it made its way up the bank. Moments later a mere scrap of kitten slipped from the tangle of brush and sat down at the road edge. The tiny female kitten upon seeing the bodies of her family lying a short distance away mewed softly, but did not move out onto the road. Sensing the tragedy at hand she sat in silence as if confused, peering at the clumps of dirty fur. The kitten like her mother was covered in long white fur, wet and dirty, shivering in the cold air. Too afraid to move the waif remained at the road edge for a time crying pitifully, the amber eyes darting about fearfully.

The kitten's vigil ended abruptly when an automobile roared by spraying her with chunks of mud and gravel. Leaping back into the brush, tumbling down the bank, she began clawing up the other side. Running scared she dashed into a field and momentarily took cover in a clump of weeds. On and on the kitten ran too terrified to stop and came to a huge oak tree near the center of the field and without hesitation darted beneath a root wad. Blindly she followed a narrow tunnel leading down beneath the old tree and came at last to a leafy burrow. She sat down, blinking rapidly mewing softly and staring up at the opening above. Daylight faded, prompting the kitten to curl up and soon she lay sleeping.

Night shadows moved across the field engulfing the oak tree and it wasn't long and darkness fell over the winter land. A crescent moon rose and beyond a myriad of stars appeared in the sky. A cold north wind rustled the branches of the tree where an owl sat carefully scanning the field below. The owl hooted from time to time, answered by another south of the road where the bodies of the female cat and the kittens lay. Coyotes began their run looking for food, passing close to the tree and then moving on. One coyote stopped briefly taking in the scent of the kitten at the entrance to the tunnel, but it soon gave up and disappeared into the darkness.

Deep beneath the tree the kitten laid gazing about in the total darkness of its hide away. Driven by hunger she got to her feet and then cautiously began the climb up to the entrance to the tunnel. She stopped, sniffing the cold air, picking up the scent of the coyote, growling deep in her throat. Instinctively she lay down in a crouching position, ears laid back. Trembling from head to toe she crawled closer to the outside and peered out into the night. A wood rat sitting on a root just outside the tree attracted her attention, the need for food irresistible, but upon hearing the rustle of leaves in the tunnel, the rodent scampered to a fallen limb lying nearby. A shadow dropped from the tree, frightening the kitten and she looked up to see the owl pick up the rat, it's mighty wings lifting it again into the tree above. The kitten darted back down the tunnel and took refuge in the musty leaves. She lay for a time listening, mewing softly. Reaching out she idly snared a leaf, toyed with it for awhile, yawning sleepily. Too weary to climb the tunnel again she curled up into a furry ball still mewing and finally drifted off into a fitful sleep.

Sometime later the kitten awakened to the sound of yipping and scratching at the entrance to the tunnel. Coyotes were trying to dig her out. Burrowing deeper under the cover of leaves she peered upward fearful of the danger that now threatened her life. She wanted to run, but there was no place to go and instinctively remained quite, listening to the frenzy of digging above her. An hour passed and quietness settled in and no longer could she smell the coyotes, but fear kept her awake the rest of the night.

The first light of dawn stole into the tunnel, gray and cold. Frost glistened brightly across the field. The old tree draped in winter's lace, its limbs empty and still. Brown leaves, remnants of summer drifted down rustling against the small opening, shutting out most of the light. From somewhere not far away came the sound of a lone running hound and the bawl of milk cows heading to a barn.

The amber eyes of the kitten wide with uncertainty peered at the entrance. She stood up, yawned and stretched. Unable to remain beneath the tree any longer in desperate need of food, she quickly climbed the steep incline to the entrance pushing her head through the leaves. Emerging slowly outside, less cautious than she should have been, was suddenly confronted by a field mouse munching on a buck brush berry. Both the mouse and the kitten were taken by surprise, but the mouse more agile quickly ran around the tree and disappeared. The kitten sat down, pretending to groom herself, looking about for the elusive rodent, but she soon gave up and began walking away from the tree in a westerly direction. Frost stung her feet and crying with every step, she ran stopping only long enough on an old post to lick her paws. Bedraggled, in dire need of food and nearing exhaustion the kitten came to a dilapidated board fence. Much of it had collapsed and lay on the ground.

The sun well above the horizon warmed the tiny body and she lay for a time sleepily looking off in the distance, unaware that a large opossum was approaching the broken line of fence searching for food. Two juvenile field mice darted out from under a board near the kitten and ran up the board she lay on. The kitten struck out with a paw armed with needle sharp claws snagging one of the mice. She quickly drew the struggling animal to her and swallowed it whole. Up and running after the second mouse, she came face to face with the opossum that in turn came at her grunting hungrily. Hissing, jumping straight up the kitten squalled and ran into the high weeds with the lumbering opossum in pursuit. Darting from the cover of high grass debris the kitten climb a post and began running down the fence, jumping from one connected board to another. The fence led to her to the road and upon hearing the sound of an automobile leaped to the ground and fled in terror across the field. The field, a broad expanse of matted grass and vines appeared endless, but on she ran and by midmorning could barely hold her head up. Doggedly she struggled on oblivious to her waning endurance.

The sound of a barking dog brought the kitten to a halt crouching low to the ground. Growling she crawled on her belly a few feet to a cluster of musk thistle. Peering through it she spied a little black dog tied on chain in front of a small building. A large barn stood near by where chickens clucked noisily. A large red rooster marched out a door of the barn strutting about. The sight of the dog and rooster were terrifying to the kitten, for never before had she seen such creatures. Hissing loudly she crouched lower into the thistle and began a slow retreat back the way she had come only to see a large white goose approaching squawking loudly. The dog jumping and running came to the end of the chain that extended at least ten foot from the small building. Bouncing high into the air the dog continued its frantic barking intensifying the drama at hand.

The kitten, her frail body trembling violently, watching the goose now dangerously close, stood up arching her back hissing menacingly trying desperately to discourage it from coming closer and began backing away from the bird. The dog realizing the kitten was closer set up a shrill howl. The kitten now cornered, gathered all the strength she could muster and headed straight for the dark entrance of the small building. She passed within a foot of the dog and sent the rooster running back into the barn; bringing forth pandemonium inside the chicken quarters. Running through the doorway of the little building, skidding across the floor hitting the back wall, the kitten collapsed in a heap of fur and glowering eyes. She lay spent of all strength, terrified of what might happen next.

The dog apprehensive of what the creature could do to him cautiously approached the doorway of his house and peeked inside. Growling, he began barking again, wagging his tail when a man appeared at the corner of the barn.

"Hey Amigo, have you got company inside?" the man asked and then knelt by the shaggy little dog.

"Bolder now, Amigo stuck his head inside the building, growling fiercely but was gently pushed aside by his master.

"You better let me take a look ole buddy," the man said. "I wouldn't want you to take on more than you can handle. My goodness Amigo, it's only a kitten and a sorrowful looking one at that. The little critter is scared half to death. I bet it's a wild thing and probably never seen a dog or human before. You stay put and I'll find a heavy glove and see if I can get a hold of the poor little thing."

A few minutes later the man returned wearing thick leather gloves. Smiling he reached inside, one hand extended toward the ragged kitten. Crying out, cowering against the wall, the kitten watched wide eyes as the hand drew closer. Shrieking now, she began swatting at the hand and growling, trying to drive it away, but to no avail.

The hand swiftly closed around the kitten, holding her gently but firmly. Ignoring the sharp teeth and claws, the man lifted her from the floor and slowly brought the distraught creature to the light of day. Overwhelmed the kitten screamed in fear and shrank deeper into the gloved hand.

The man held the struggling kitten out of reach of Amigo, smiling. "Why it's a female kitten," the man said. "Come now little one, don't be afraid, no harm will come to you. "What a beautiful gift for the wife on Christmas Eve. "Christmas, yes that will be your name."

Strangely the kitten, or rather Christmas sensed her captor meant no harm and ceased struggling. He gently thrust her inside his coat and seconds later she snuggled deep inside the warmth of the garment and began purring contentedly.

"My dear," said the man to a woman standing inside the kitchen of their home, "one of God's creatures has come to us seeking shelter, food and a home."

"Oh no not another baby opossum," she laughed.

"No," he smiled. "Her name is Christmas, a bit of an angel I suspect."

Gently the man removed Christmas from the coat, holding her up. The kitten somewhat bewildered by it all gazed timidly about the large room, strangely scented and wonderfully warm. The woman placed a bowl of warm milk on the floor. The journey across the field was over and would soon be forgotten, for in this house she would become a queen.

THE END

Lucky Seven

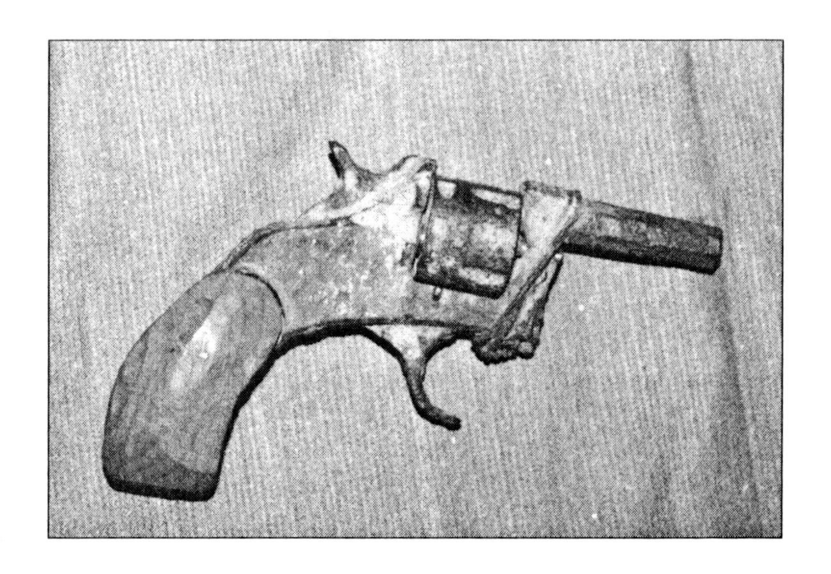

Frozen in rust, Author's photograph of a seven shot revolver, (Lucky Seven) excavated from a cave on the Niangua River.

Lucky Seven

It was one of those hot, hazy August mornings that often obscures the sun for an hour or two and few people were about. I had just stepped out of Ed Chigger's Café, trying to make up my mind whether or not I needed a shave, when I spied a stranger riding slowly along Front Street of Hanley, Missouri.

The Stranger a tall man, or so it appeared, clean shaven with shoulder length gray black hair and wearing a dusty riding coat and hat. He sat astride a leggy dark roan stallion. The man rode with head down as if preoccupied, looking neither left nor right, but I sensed the fellow was very much aware of his surroundings especially the street.

My two years as town marshal had taught me if nothing else to pay close attention to strangers in town. I moved closer to the edge of the boardwalk and watched the stallion high step past the café and come to a halt in front of the Union Hotel. The stranger dismounted, shed the riding coat and tucked it behind the saddle and tied the roan to a hitching post. Looking up he slowly scanned the street, his gaze briefly settling on me.

The year was 1883 and Hanely was still rebuilding from the devastation left in the wake of a vicious band of Baldnobbers one summer night during the final days of the Civil War. They came thirty men strong armed with new fangled repeating rifles, intent on destroying the Yankee town and outlying areas. The unholy bunch of renegades killed and maimed more than fifty people. Two women claimed to have been assaulted by some of the men.

The Baldnobbers set fire to a goodly portion of the town after they took everything of value. They whooped and hollered profanities for the better part of an hour, killing or wounding any man or woman who tried to defend the town.

Pa was one of the unfortunate defenders shot dead. I was too young to remember that dreadful night, but grew up listening to the horrid tales of death and destruction. Years of hardships followed, but Ma and me managed to get by. We worked from sunup to sundown on our forty acre farm, located about mile west of town.

Ma died in the autumn of 1880, two weeks before my twenty-first birthday. I laid her to rest next to Pa in the south corner of an orchard back of the house. I'd had enough and rode into town with the intentions of never returning to the farm, but two events changed my mind. The first was the town marshal's job offered to me at thirty a month and found. I accepted the job without hesitation.

The second and most memorable event came about a little over a couple of weeks later when I saw Polly Ann for the first time. Although I did not realize how much she would eventually change my entire outlook on life. She was a new comer in town working in the High Ridge Saloon as a part time barmaid and pianist. A beautiful mite of a woman, with eyes as pure blue as the sky and hip length hair the color of ginger red.

Polly walked with a slight limp and I later learned she had when very young fallen from a run away horse and broken her ankle. But as far as I was concerned the impairment did not deprive her of a God given grace and beauty. I immediately fell in love with her.

A week later I saw Polly again and was so taken with my feelings for her I came dangerously close stepping out in front of a fast moving team of horses. I had enough wits about me to jump back in time, but stumbled and fell into a muddy pool of water. I sat there feeling like a fool.

"You should watch where you're going Marshal," said a soft voice teasingly. "You could have been killed."

Startled and blushing to the hilt I looked up into Polly's smiling face. Even then, while setting in the pool looking rather ridiculous I was speechless and in awe at the beauty of the girl above me. The stunning face would have put an angel to shame and the eyes and lace open at her throat rendered me as helpless as a baby chick standing in neck deep water.

I watched in silence as she bent down removing a dainty white handkerchief from a sleeve of her dress. She proceeded to wipe the mud from my face, all the while gazing mischievously into my eyes. She stood up, tucked the now soiled hanky back into the sleeve and walked away. I reckon I would still be sitting there if she hadn't turned and called out to me.

"Marshal, you better get up before you are run over," she laughed. "You take care now and watch where you're going."

The stranger eyed me rather closely, turned and entered the hotel. I didn't like the looks of the man, but said nothing and headed for the barbershop for a shave. When I arrived I found the place a buzz with talk of the stranger. Word as usual had spread quickly across town. It seemed as if everyone there was trying to get a word in. I sat down in a barber chair and above the din of voices heard Evert Ballard's voice ring out above them all.

"That feller is J.W. Haston!" Evert declared. "If you-all will shut up for a minute I'll tell you about him"

Evert, the proprietor of one of the mercantile stores in town and former deputy sheriff was respected by most folks and silence quickly filled the room.

Evert cussed a big one and said. "It's been a long time but I remember the man as if it was yesterday. He was one of the men who robbed the bank in town about fifteen years ago. We killed two of the gang, but J.W. and three others got away."

"I reckon I'll have a talk with Mister Haston,' I replied, motioning for Ben Holt to get on with my shave.

"Isaac Cunningham you had better be careful," Evert cautioned sternly. "Ain't no doubt you got your Grandpa Henry's size and grit, but you're just a county boy. I reckon you ain't no match against the gun hand of J. W. Haston. Take my advice and deputize a couple of men with shotguns when you face that rascal, you might live longer."

"I appreciate your concern Mister Ballard," I replied gruff like and stood up. "I expect I can take care of myself."

"Be careful son," he answered.

Long about ten o' clock that morning I spotted J. W. coming out of the hotel and decided it was a good time to confront the man. I met him near the center of the street and he did not appear as tall as I first took him to be. He stopped a few from me, eying the badge I wore on the front of my shirt. He appeared pleasant enough with rather sharp features for a man of his age. The eyes betrayed a shadowed alertness that caused me a bit of concern.

It was during my scrutiny of him I noticed a pearl handled Colt protruding from a belt drawn around his waste.

"Are you J.W. Haston?" I asked a bit too loudly.

The eyes lit up ever so slightly and he nodded. "Yeah that's my name." he answered real friendly like.

"I got reason to suspect you may be wanted by the law. I would appreciate you accompanying me to the jail."

"J 'W. glanced to the left and right and dang he walked away, completely ignoring me. He stopped a few feet from the boardwalk and turned around. "Am I under arrest?"

"No Mister Haston," I answered. "I want to check the wanted posters against your description and if you ain't on them, you're free to go."

"I ain't wanted for nothing, including the bank robbery here in town," he replied patiently. "Turned state evidence and got off without serving any time. I'm just passing through on my way to Morris Texas."

"Nevertheless Mister Haston," I said feeling a bit riled, "I'm ordering you to accompany me to the jail. If what you say is true we'll clear this up real quick."

"J.W. took a couple steps toward me, his head slightly bowed. The thumb of his right hand now hooked in the belt next to the Colt. The friendly expression on his face had not changed when he looked up, regarding me intently.

Pa's old cap and ball Colt of which I carried at the time was barely visible in the waste band of my trousers and instinctively I reached for it.

I have yet today seen a hand move as quickly as Haston's did for in less than the blink of an eye I was looking down the muzzle of a short barrel Colt forty five. I had yet to touch the butt of Pa's gun.

"Believe me Marshal, I don't want any trouble with you, he said pleasant like, "but I ain't going with you. I want only to be left alone."

I could only shake my head in disbelief at the unexpected turn of events. Mister Ballard had been right. "I understand," I said, "but it's my duty to take you in. "I'm gonna draw my weapon and I reckon you will have to shoot me if you can."

It was at this time Polly Ann arrived on the scene and without a word she stepped between us. She glanced up at me and smiled, drew a deep breath and looked toward J. W. real serious like and frowned.

"You ain't shooting the man I plan on marrying," she said calmly, but with determination.

I'm not certain who was the more taken back by Polly's statement. J'W., stood gaping at her, but the Colt remained steady in his hand.

"Polly step out of the way, please," I said.

"No!" she answered. "J.W. Haston put that pistol back in your belt or I'll shoot you!"

Haston glanced at me as if confused and appeared to have lost a bit of his composure and then he grinned. "No Missy I ain't putting my gun down. This is none of your business."

"Isaac," Polly said to me, "this doesn't mean I'm going to have a flock of kids, plow behind a mule from sunup to sundown for a pot of beans."

"Polly Ann please, uh, step out…." I stammered.

She once again leveled her gaze at Haston and said sweetly," "Hush Isaac, I love you."

Slowly she raised her right arm to bear on Haston and I flinched at the sunlight glinting off the barrel of a small pistol in her hand. Before I could say another word, the bantam revolver cracked sharply, followed by five more rounds, all missing their intended victim.

Haston stepped back, his face chalk white, the gun in his hand drooping a bit. To my surprise Polly again squeezed the trigger and low and behold the gun fired again. The bullet hit Haston's Colt, ricocheting upward striking the man's forehead a glancing blow. He dropped like a poled steer and lay deathly still sort of peaceful like.

I quickly went to Polly, astonished at the capacity of the gun dangling from her limp hand. I had never heard of a seven shot revolver let alone seen one.

"It's called a Lucky Seven," she whispered. "Did I kill him Isaac? I really didn't want to."

"I believe you did," I answered taking the gun from her hand. "He should have put the gun back in the belt."

Polly nodded and made an attempt to smile, but instead fainted in my arms.

Polly and I were married about two weeks later and we moved to the farm Ma had left me. She bore two children, a son and daughter. The years past so quickly it seemed, but we prospered and by the time the children were grown we had acquired four hundred acres along the Dousinberry Creek.

Polly passed away a year ago today at the age of eighty nine and although time had faded the sun from her hair and dimmed those beautiful blue eyes, she remained strong willed and devoted to me and the children.

Today while going through her things I found the Lucky Seven Revolver. Oh by the way, J. W. Haston was only wounded in the fracas and served five years in the Missouri Sate Pen, of which he deserved. He came back one day an old man weary in spirit and body. Polly insisted we take him in and gave him the room over the kitchen. J. W. remained with us until his death ten years later working long hours on the farm. There was little he wouldn't have done for Polly and the kids. One of the last things he said to me before he died, "I had no intentions of shooting you that day, I was only bluffing." and he laughed.

THE END

The Return Of Jake Latimer

Death at time takes place unexpectedly, an unfortunate event so to speak, possibly leaving the most menial tasks incomplete. These uncompleted tasks will go undone unless a friend or family member deems it necessary to do them, such as slopping the hogs, or milking the cows. But of course in reality it does not concern the deceased, or perhaps it does, for pride may reach beyond the grave. And so it was on that warm spring morning of Jake Latimer's demise.

Jake was widower, a tall man, slightly bent, but agile for his age of eighty seven years and handsome. Although most of his hair had lost the deep brown of his youth, it still remained a thick mat of curls turning the eyes of local single women and a few of the married ones. The old man's eyes were bright, clear and a deep sultry brown that often brought sighs from the opposite sex. He could still follow the hounds ahead of many of the younger men.

Most folks were unaware that he wore store bought teeth, especially the women in his life. Jake was farmer and the father of nine children and a host of grand and great grand children.

Jake rose early as usual on that fateful day with intentions of completing the cultivation of a patch of corn in the creek bottom, then ride horseback into town approximately twelve miles. Later in the evening he planned to hitch the buggy to one of his finest geldings and go courting a lady friend, escorting her to a square dance where he played the fiddle. He anticipated it would be a delightful evening, except for the store bought teeth that were down right uncomfortable, but of course he would not have been caught dead without them.

Jake whistled merrily as he waited for a kettle of water to heat, admiring his reflection in the mirror. Soon he filled a granite pan with steaming water and pored a little into a small crock bowl. Frowning he removed the dentures and placed them carefully in the bowl to soak while he shaved.

Sometime later he finished the shave after inspecting every inch of the well preserved face for stray stubble. He set the shaving mug on a shelf along with the razor and reached for the teeth, but alas, Father Time laid a heavy hand on Jake's shoulder and he collapsed and died before he hit the floor.

Jake was quite well known throughout the county and folks came from miles around to pay their last respects. Many were family members living on adjoining farms along the Niangua River. The line of mourners extended well beyond a mile behind the horse drawn hearse on the road to the Lone Rock Church.

It was a fine funeral as far as funerals go, with a heap of flowers filling the front of the little church. A blue, brass trimmed casket contained the body, laid out in a black suite, white shirt and tie. A large diamond encrusted gold ring adorned a finger of his right hand that would be removed prior to closing the casket and given to his only surviving sister.

Martha Pitts, Jake's current lady friend stood at the head of the casket weeping. The old woman of eighty six years had walked five miles to be there, leaning against a flower stand with head bowed in exhaustion. Most people shuffling past the casket ignored the woman openly disapproving her presence.

After filing past Jake, all gathered outside near the open grave quietly discussing the elaborate casket and abundance of flowers, but a few voiced remarks about how gaunt Jake appeared, unlike the robust man they once knew.

Later that day after Jake had been laid to rest next to his wife Ida Mae, the family gathered at the home place. The big oak table in the dining room brimmed with an abundance of food left their by friends and neighbors.

The descendants of Jake and Ida said a short prayer of thanks and then nosily gathered about the table filling their plates with fried chicken, ham, mashed potatoes and red eye gravy and whatever else they could pile on the plate. They sat down and the feast began in earnest.

Carroll Sue the youngest of the nine children was the only sibling not eating and instead stood alone in the washroom by the stand weeping softly. She wiped her eyes and gazed about the room, avoiding the floor where Jake had been found. She looked tearfully at the shaving mug and razor, placed there by her father. Below them sat the small crock bowl containing Jake's dentures.

"Oh my God," she wailed, "Papa is without his teeth!"

Everyone looked up in disbelief at the bowl in Carroll's trembling hand.

"That's the reason why Pa looked so gaunt," Carl J. mumbled through a mouthful of pink angel food cake. "He sure didn't like being seen without them."

"Well it's too late now," a younger brother piped up chewing on a drumstick.

Carroll shrugged, set the bowl down and joined the others at the table. And it wasn't long and the feast was again in full swing, smacking and grunting. Little more was said for several minutes as the family partook of the food.

Sometime later the screen door opened rather abruptly and everyone looked up to see who it was entering the house so rudely. Spoons, forks and plates cluttered to the floor and Sarah, Jakes only sister gasped and slumped back in a dead faint. The rest watched in silence as Jake strode past them and entered the wash room. He did not say a word and plucked the store bought teeth from the bowl and popped them into his mouth. He turned then, appearing as handsome as ever and swaggered out the door.

THE END

White Buffalo

They bore the child to the Mountain of the Sun after only five years of life, not to be laid to rest, but to fulfill the destiny of the Indian Nations. A strong lad with hair as white as the snow, eyes as clear and blue as the sky and skin the color of copper, an Indian true in spirit and body. Within his breast beat a heart as pure and innocent as the first breath of spring.

The Mountain of the Sun obscured, stood alone among a chain of mountains as old as time occupying a broken nation within a nation where deceit, greed, waste and treachery reigned supreme. Its lofty peaks reached high above tranquil clouds and caught the sun from the east and west, flaring at times like burning embers, beguiling the eye. It was as if no one saw the magnificent peak, for on it no human had yet to tread.

They the people, chosen ones, named the boy White Buffalo for in him was yet to awaken the prophecies given the Indian in the beginning. Within the lad there awaited wisdom, strength, endurance and faith to serve him all the days of his life. Those who bore the boy up the Mountain of the Sun, questioned not why, nor whether he would survive, for they were of unshakable faith and knew he would find the answers for his survival in the wind, in the flames dancing at his hearth, the four seasons and the bounty of the mountain.

White Buffalo would not be lonely, but solitude would be a constant companion, to taunt him and try to erode all the virtues of his soul. He would know no fear, but fear would be there lurking in the shadows to strike out unexpectedly to try and send him fleeing to cower before his fire.

They the people who bore him to the mountain returned four times, once in each passing season, not to interfere, but in reverence, to strengthen their own faith, then left never to return again, for they perished in the wilderness below. Severed of all ties to the world, White Buffalo continued to thrive oblivious of his purpose alone on the Mountain of the Sun.

It was perhaps the obscurity of the Mountain of the Sun or Devine Intervention that prohibited people from finding their way up the mysterious pinnacle of stone and earth. It could have been the seemingly endless maze of canyons and ravines surrounding the great mountain, easily confusing and destroying many a foolish human, preventing them from conquering the world of White Buffalo.

Great trees of timeless origin stood on the mountain, unscathed by the axe and saw and below them flourished all forms of beasts and birds, completely free of the dangers from extinction that prevailed across the land and world below the mountain. The view from the cave where White Buffalo lived lay around him unspoiled by roads and buildings and he knew nothing of such intrusive inanimate objects. The forest was so dense the sun could only penetrate the edges of the wall of mighty trees. The four seasons were not blemished or degraded by man's contaminates shrouding the land below the mountain.

Time past and White Buffalo grew stronger in mind and body, wise beyond his years. Content to wander about the mountain, taking food only when the need arose, kneeling in respect at the side of an elk or deer he slew to give thanks. One particular spring day as clear and fresh as the Creator meant it to be, White Buffalo found himself at the edge of a cliff, jutting out from the mountain. He stood for a time gazing out over a wide expanse of land lying in all directions. The wind brought to him an awful stench, nothing like he had ever known before. The wind also carried the faint cries of fear and uncertainty. Bewildered by what he saw, heard and smelled he hurried back up the mountain to the cave. Below there were forests dead and dieing, rivers bloated and fouled with the excretion of humanity and worst of all the apathy of mankind. Too confused and troubled by the experience he did not return to the cliff for many years, deliberately avoiding the trail that led there.

One hundred years later after White Buffalo's arrival on the Mountain of the Sun, the wind brought to him one night a song. The Indian listened intently for he had never heard such sounds. He began chanting ancient words, long forgotten by those of his species and slowly turned toward the east. There was a rhythm in the song he could not ignore, tugging at his heart, mind and soul. A persistent force drawing him to the words flowing from the wind and chanting louder and louder he began understanding the meaning of the song. The message revealed, chilled him to the core. It felt as if his soul was being wretched from him and stood trembling not in fear but in awe of the power at hand. He stood gazing toward the east and for the remainder of the day and following night did not move a muscle.

When at last the dawn came, bathing him in scarlet hues and gentle warmth, he turned, stumbled inside the cave, but not to rest, a wretched figure of a man completely nude. The intensity of the blue eyes grew brighter, reflecting the light of flames suddenly rising from the hearth. The flames beckoned him and he began dancing to their rhythm. Chanting not words, but sounds likened to the coyote and all the creatures of the forests, mountains and prairies. White Buffalo moved to the center of the cave. Faster and faster he danced with the flames, held firmly in the spell cast upon him. Hour after hour he danced with the light, stepping high, bending low, face contorted, teeth barred. On through the day he danced, the forest resounding with his cries of agony. Night crept across the mountain reaching the cave and White Buffalo collapsed near the dieing embers of the fire and lay as if in death.

White Buffalo lay for two days in a dreamless stupor and on the eve of the second day awakened. The ashes in the hearth were cold, but seconds later flames miraculously rose up. Shadows or so it appeared began appearing on the walls around him. He quickly discovered they were not shadows, but spirits from the underworld the gateway to the universe and beyond, the place of the beginning. Silently they gathered around, cleansing him in the essence of cedar smoke, and laid at his feet clothing to wear. One by one the spirits called his name and foretold of coming events. Great fountains of fire would erupt from the mountains around the world and tidal waves of greater magnitude than ever known would sweep arcos the land destroying those humans of all race creed and color that should not have been and finally the cleansing of Mother Earth. The devastation would equal only that of the Great Flood.

Several days later, White Buffalo stood on a high pinnacle of stone, gazing apprehensively out over the Mountain of the Sun, feeling very much alone. Long gray white hair lay tightly braided across one shoulder. Elk skin britches, vest and moccasins clothed the old man. He stood straight and tall against the vast expanse of land before him.

The mountains around White Buffalo were drab, barren and lifeless. The Mountain of the Sun no longer obscured stood shinning like a beacon for all to see. Sighing deeply he made his way slowly down off the stone and began a long trek to the edge of the wide canyon he had visited several years before.

Many hours later at daybreak he stood on the rim of the wide canyon. The sky a tinted overcast pulsated strangely. A cold wind blew across the great chasm and he shivered. The ground beneath him shuddered, but unafraid quickly regained his footing. He could see below the floor of the canyon rising and falling, dislodging huge chunks of the walls. In the distance far, far away he could see though eyes equal only to those of an eagle, ominous clouds of dark smoke rising from the cities. They had begun to crumble, falling into wide deep glowing chasms soon to be swallowed up. The Earth around him began wailing, groaning, spitting fire and plumes of smoke. Highways buckled, turning upside down crushing the multitudes of humans fleeing toward the Mountain of the Sun. Rivers turned into steam, disappeared, then reappeared flooding the land with sea water. Mountains toppled, filling the valleys with molten lava. Prairies were cast upward and soon were mountains glowing red from within. Day became night as dust and ash swept aside the sunlight. The seas rose steadily, rushing over great portions of the land. The Earth trembled from pole to pole and it seemed there would be no end to the catastrophic events unleashed on the world and its creatures.

White Buffalo stood weeping, watching as millions of people swarmed like pestilence toward the base of the mountain. He saw a sea of humanity driven by fear and desperation, seeking safety on the high peak above them only to be trampled by others. On and on they poured into the canyon, torn, bleeding, mortally wounded, they began clawing up the face of the cliff. Their cries of fear and pain buzzed around White Buffalo like a swarm of angry bees. Wave after wave perished in the deep canyon and still they came.

It seemed to White Buffalo, all would perish, but one by one brothers and sisters of flesh and soul inched their way up the treacherous cliff. He marveled at their courage and stamina as they reached the crest of the wall and crawled toward him. When at last he reckoned no one else would be coming, White Buffalo beckoned to the three hundred sixteen men and women representing all the clans of Earth to rise to their feet. Silently they obeyed and two by two followed him up the Mountain of the Sun.

The story of White Mountain is old and varies in flavor, intensity and dogma, handed down from many generations and is fortified it is said by a vision of a man bearing nail scars in his hands. This story is a figment of my imagination and came to be when inspired by an old man of Siouan heritage who often teased me with tales of old.

THE END

And On The Sixth Day

It is said in the Good Book, that God created the heavens, the earth, the creatures of the land, sea and air and finally created man in his own image. I have often wondered which animal he created first, especially the dog and horse, knowing full well these two animals would be man's best friend. I have no way of knowing for certain and after considerable thought on the matter decided the dog won out and was the first to be created. Another dilemma faced God, which breed of dog to make first, the poodle, I think not, although they are precious. The rat terror would have been a good choice, for they are spunky little fellers and great squirrel hunters, but not likely the first. The sixth day must have been a long one as God pondered over the small mound of dirt at his feet. The collie was very likely at the top of his list for the love and devotion instilled in this beautiful animal is truly an inspiration of our Creator, however, I think the collie came in a close second. I believe he envisioned something else, smiled, and then gently touched the mound of dirt and watched as the first long eared, bony framed, gentle eyed black and tan hound raised its magnificent head and bawled. God, pleased with the results quickly fashioned another, a mate for the first. It didn't take long for him to realize these beautiful creatures were without purpose and set about making the opossum, raccoon, squirrel, bear and a host of other animals the black and tans love to trail.

I believe the idea of creating something in his own image came about shortly after the hounds, so pleased was he with them he wanted to share the dogs with others who would appreciate the finer qualities of such an animal. The hounds also needed a place to live when not out trailing critters. The bawl of these hounds was beautiful music to his ears and thought it would be sad not to have someone to sit back and listen to the sound drifting up from a deep hollow or beneath a huge oak tree on a high ridge or watch the dogs run a fox across a river bottom field. It would have to be someone who would tolerate the smelly creatures, keep the ticks off them and be willing to follow the hounds wherever they went. The angels were too busy and much to refined to ever take up hunting with the hounds.

And so it came to be that God created a man (Adam) in his own image, instilling in him a deep love and respect for all animals, especially the black and tan hounds. He again faced another dilemma, for soon after Adam came to be, God saw that his flesh and blood image was as equally pleased with the hounds, but he quickly realized Adam desired only to follow the dogs into the wilderness to hunt. This would not do, for Adam could not fritter away his time in the woods hunting. God smiled, and created a mate for his likeness and called her "Eve."

God fixed up an old shack in the middle of a beautiful track of land and named it the Garden of Eden. A wide clear river flowed through it with high grass meadows and tall trees. It was a place of unimaginable bounty where the hounds could run and hunt the critters thriving there. He called to Adam and Eve, along with the hounds and showed them their new home. Adam was delighted as was Eve, but she wasn't so pleased with the hounds. She didn't particularly like the dogs, but was kind to them and agreed to let them sleep on the porch so long as they were not tick and flea infected. Content to be Adams mate, she worked hard about the little homestead, growing potatoes, corn and squash and canning most of it in Mason glass jars. Adam the head of the household milked the cows, cut brush from the lower forty and carried water from the river.

Hunting was rather limited in Eden and it wasn't long and just about every opossum, raccoon and squirrel took off for parts unknown to find a quieter place to live away from the feisty hounds. The hounds soon grew discontented with only chipmunks and wood rats to trail and began to stray into the hills. Adam could hear them running, bawling, having the time of their lives. He slipped off one evening with the dogs and this did not set well with Eve. She asked God what to do and he smiled and said not to worry for Adam was a responsible man and would eventually grow tired of hunting with the black and tans.

God cautioned Eve about trying to discourage Adam from being with the hounds and especially forbade her to tempt him with a fresh baked apple pie. "The Earth has many kinds of dirt." he said. "The dirt I made Adam from is Missouri dirt and to fetch him an apple pie would be a mistake, for he would want more and more of the delicacy."

Eve was not convinced and so a few days later with the faint bawl of the hounds ringing in her ears, she baked an apple pie. Long about sunrise Adam and the hounds returned, weary of the long night, hungry and in need of rest. Now Adam was a true hound dog man and before he entered the shack he picked all the ticks off the dogs, fed them a generous portion of pork rind, turnip greens for bulk and bedded them down on the porch. He sat for a time stroking each head and singing quietly to them. All the while watching from the door, Eve kept the apple pie warm in the oven.

When at last the black and tans lay asleep, Adam went into the shack; his overalls caked with river mud and stank much like his beloved hounds. Eve stood waiting at the table a devilish gleam in her eyes and sat before him a generous slab of apple pie. He quickly ate the piece and called for more and she again handed him another slab about half the pie. He called for more and she slid the rest of it across the table, quite pleased with his appetite and watched as he consumed the rest of the forbidden fruit and then sat back contentedly and belched.

Adam was not as innocent as it might appear, for he knew God did not want him eating apple pie. He knew not why, only that it was forbidden. Like all true hounds' men, Adam after a long hunt never turned down fried chicken, mashed potatoes and gravy and now apple pie. Worried that God would find out, he reluctantly agreed to limit hunting to two nights a week if Eve would continue baking pies for him. The couple swore not to tell God, but as it is well known, he knows all and a few days later he sent Adam and Eve packing along with the hounds.

God told Adam he would have to start from scratch and work hard to make a living. Adam was devastated for he knew this would take precious time away from the hounds. Eve was told she would now bear Adam's children and as strange as it may seem, encouraged her to keep baking apple pies.

The rest is history except for one little known fact. Adam and Eve crossed the Red River, made their way through Kingston, Arkansas where he and Eve visited for a time with a cousin with the Wright name and finally settled down on McKee

Ridge a little south of the Niangua River in Missouri. Adam built a cabin overlooking the river where a trail led down to a forest of oak trees where the biggest raccoons west of the Mississippi River thrived. He split rails for a living and took up fiddling, but on Saturday night he and his only son out of fourteen daughters headed out to the hills to follow the hounds up and down the Niangua River basin.

God made man in his image and gave him the ability to talk, laugh and cry. He instilled in us joy, sadness, grief, imagination, reasoning and most important a sense of humor. All of these aspects of man are not unique to us, but are also a part of God. To deny even one of theses virtues is to question our Creator's wisdom. Take away one and life is not what it should be, for all of them are a part of God.

THE END

An 1890's outhouse succumbing to time

Cold Seats And Spider Webs

In 1950, if I remember correctly, the remaining area south of Long Lane, Missouri, received electricity. The glow of light bulbs became a part of just about every rural home and until then I never realized how close some of the neighbors were. But standing on the front porch of my parents' house one evening, I could see the lights burning brightly in many windows across the countryside. It was a miraculous event for this fifteen year old boy who knew little about the world around him.

Perhaps one of the last things to fade in memory from the days before rural electrification was the outhouses, small buildings constructed for but one purpose to potty in. I suppose there are few if any that have any particular historical value, for they were not built as a thing of beauty and most did not endure very long setting over a shallow pit, clinging to a steep slope, succumbing to neglect.

Outhouses, for a time following rural electricity remained in use, partly because of economics and partly because some people were hesitant to have the equivalent of the privy inside their home. Strange as it may seem, a few especially the elderly considered the flush toilet standing inside the house unnatural and unhealthy and continued using the building out back along with the Sears Roebuck catalog for wiping.

Outhouses or privies as they were commonly known were rarely attractive buildings and just as rarely ever constructed for comfort. A hole cut in an oak board to sit over sufficed, for only moments were spent inside the building. Most privies had but one opening or seat for adults, however, some boasted two seats, one for the adults and a low one for the children.

These necessary buildings were constructed of a variety of materials, quite often of scrap lumber, metal sheeting, logs and a few of stone; all ideally setting over a pit that became shallower with each passing month. Their locations also varied, but generally were located several feet behind the house, preferably on a down hill slope. Iris and holly hock thrived around these outcast buildings providing succulent nectar for honey bees, bumble bees and humming birds. The pesky bees darting from plant to plant brought terror to many a young child running a gantlet though the flowers to get to the privy.

Many of the outhouses were located near a chicken yard, where the clucking and scratching of a hen or two was a common sound beneath the seat. Brush and or high horse weeds obscured many of the privies and were usually in the embrace of an ivy or wild grape vine, where spiders flourished feeding on the insects caught in their deadly webs.

The buildings were nearly always in need of repair, leaky roofs, doors that had long since given up their hinges and conspicuous gaps in the sides back and front were common. Like the leaning Tower of Pisa, so were many of these buildings, often propped up with a spilt post or rail. Unlike today, a guest might say, "You have a beautiful bathroom."

The privies of yesterday were not a subject to talk about with anyone, let alone company.

The outhouse was a haven for blacksnakes, the dreaded Copper Head and the mighty King snake. The buildings harbored scorpions, wasps, hornets and a wide variety of spiders, including the menacing Wolf spider, but nevertheless the little building was a place of comfort in the lives of rural folks.

Outhouses or privies often were the victim of Halloween, especially those around schools and churches. It was common for a building to be turned upside down, hauled off to a new location and not unusual to be placed on top of a church or school. There once stood an outhouse behind the Windyville general store that had been built around a tree. The reason for this odd location was because of others taken by Halloween pranksters.

The buildings simply disappeared, perhaps thrown into the river or a deep hollow and if found were several miles away. The disgruntled store owner, tired of losing the outhouses, constructed one around an oak tree and it remained there for several years finally succumbing to age.

When I was a young lad I always looked forward to helping clear the wasps from the Brushy Ridge School outhouses. Usually a week before school commenced, in the latter part of August, several families would gather at the old one room schoolhouse and ready it for the children. The building set in a clearing on a ridge above Dousinberry Creek. Taking possession of the outhouses was left to the boys and a battle ensued.

Nearly always, the privies were inhabited by large nests of red wasps, the most aggressive of their kind. But of course most boys were equally aggressive or so we thought. A fierce running battle took place and inevitably there were casualties on both sides, dead and wounded wasps lying about and boys running to their mothers with swollen lips, noses, hands and arms. It was a time to freely enter the girl's outhouse to make a show of bravery to any of the fair ones watching.

But of course the wasps were driven from the buildings, secured for another season, to again become a haven for anything that came along. Weathered gray, sagging a bit, these two old buildings stood next to the timber for several years until the closing of the Brushy Ridge School.

Perhaps the most ignored and less appreciated, least talked about, the outhouses of the yesterdays are an important aspect of American heritage. They contained secrets I'm certain that will never been known. I'm sure many a man or woman, boy or girl sat leafing through a Sears Roebuck catalog dreaming of a new pair of shoes, a dress or a shirt or a double set of Lash Luru cap pistols and a box of caps.

They were quite places of dignity, though humble, where one could make plans to get even with an uppity city cousin or read for a while from "Penrod and Sam," not to mention looking for the choice wiping paper in the catalog. They are not buildings I wish to revisit, but at least the memories are there and that is close enough.

THE END

Author's woodcarving of a Civil War Soldier

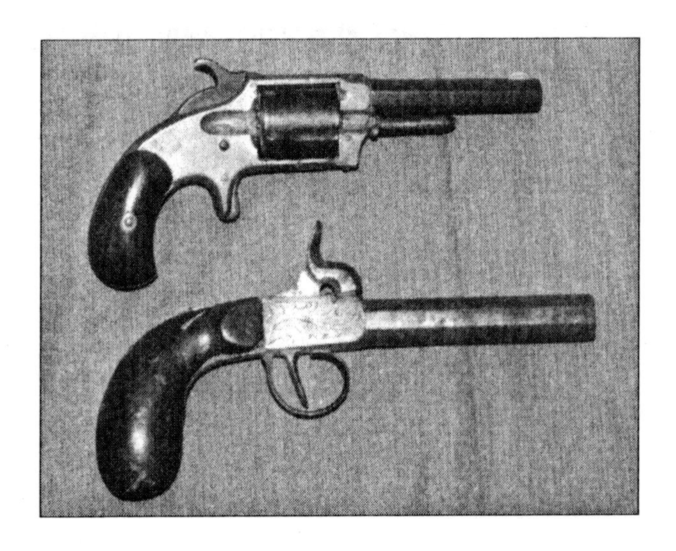

Original hideout pistols, from the 1800's: including the Civil War Era.

In The Shade Of An Oak

There is a lone tombstone standing a short distance off Highway 64 near the old town of Plad, Missouri. A grey stone, weathered with age, obscured by brush and vine, shrouded in the shade of a huge oak tree. The stone marks the spot where a young Confederate soldier lies at rest. The following story honors this fallen man and all the other brave soldiers who perished in the Civil War.

Not long after sunrise on August 7, 1861, twenty two mounted men of the Fifth Missouri, Confederate Militia, rode slowly along a narrow dirt road, approximately fifteen miles northeast of Buffalo. Saddle weary and in need of food the soldiers armed with an assortment of common rifles and dressed in butternut gray moved in relative silence along the shadowy tree lined trace.

Captain Billy Clarkson rode at the head of the thin line of men, a stanch defender of the Confederacy, keeping a wary eye on the road ahead. He caught the flare of a match to his left and turned to see Private Josh Elam lighting his pipe. The Captain immediately halted his mount, glaring at the young man of no more than eighteen years of age.

"Private," the Captain whispered loudly, "put that pipe out. "You want to get us all killed?'

"No Sir," answered Private Elam.

"Don't let it happen again or I'll throw the pipe into the brush and I reckon you ain't gonna like that."

A mile or so on the soldiers came to a small farmhouse located near the road side. Setting on the front porch was a large basket of corn yet to be shucked. Roasting ears, sweet and tender and enough to ease the hunger pain of the men. The windows of the house were dark and the curtains drawn. A red bone hound lay on the porch, eying the strangers suspiciously but did not move or make a sound.

The Captain motioned for the soldiers to dismount and with the exception of two of the men, who remained with the horses, followed him through the gate into the yard. They quietly surrounded the house waiting for further instructions. The hound growled, jumped to his feet and ran to a nearby shed.

The Captain, accompanied by Private Elam, each with drawn revolvers stepped upon the porch. Elam was about to pick up the basket of corn when the front door opened and an old man clad only in his underwear appeared. The man, either unaware of the two men on the porch or unable to see clearly boldly stepped out the door. Captain Clarkson whirled about striking the old gentleman across the head with his revolver. Reeling backwards against the door frame cursing loudly, wiping blood from his forehead, the man then tried to reenter the house.

"Come here old man or I'll blow your head off," ordered the Captain.

The man blinded by the blood flowing from his head staggered forward and dropped to his knees. The captain pulled the old man to his feet and then shoved him off the porch. Clarkson, followed by Elam quickly entered the house. Scanning the cluttered room, the Captain saw an old woman standing in the doorway of the kitchen clothed in a nightgown, trembling from head to toe.

"Sit down in that chair over there," he ordered the woman. "We're not going to hurt you. We need food and I reckon you can spare some."

"We don't have much," she replied.

"Shut up and keep quite." said the Captain. "You don't have a choice. Are there anyone else in the house?"

"No," she answered. "What have you done to my husband Clifford? Have you killed him?"

"He's out front with the rest of my men," replied the Captain. "Private, search the house and if you find anyone else we'll burn it. I'll take the kitchen."

Less than five minutes later, shouldering a gunny sack containing two loaves of bread and several glass jars of fruit, the Captain and Elam left the house. Elam carried two shotguns and a can of gun powder. The old woman sat weeping uncontrollably in a high back rocking chair near the kitchen door. Clifford now standing against a fence post, a rifle barrel pressed tightly to his chest called out loudly. "What have you done to Emma?"

"Awe she's alright Clifford," Elam replied, handing the weapons to one of the men. "We'll be on our way shortly and I would advise to keep your mouth shut. The Captain ain't in a very good mood what with all the chiggers and ticks we've been though since last night."

Clifford's face aflame with rage, began cursing vehemently, turning eyes wide with hatred toward Captain Clarkson. "You filthy cowardly Rebels ain't fit to live!"

The Captain laid the gunny sack down and stomped over to where Clifford stood. "I'm telling you old man to shut up."

"Awe Captain, he's just scared and letting off some steam," said Elam.

"You mind your on business Private and get that food ready to travel!"

"Mister I've met some low down cowards in my day, but you are the worst," said Clifford to the Captain. "Any one that would go into a man's home and scare a woman and steal food is as low as a snake's belly."

The Captain stepped to within a foot of Clifford and ordered a couple of men to hold him tightly. He removed from his belt a sheath knife and cut a hole through Clifford's lower jaw. Screaming in agony, the old man slumped back. Quicker than the blink of an eye the Captain grabbed the man's tongue and stuffed it through the hole and then pulled it down as far as he could. Choking on blood, Clifford was let ago and fell on his knees, gagging on the blood.

"Stepping back, the Captain said. "I told you to keep your mouth shut."

"Captain that wasn't necessary," Elam cried.

"Private, you better shut up and get to your horse and mount up," ordered Clarkson.

Sometime later with their booty tied on saddles; the Fifth Missouri left the main road about a mile from Plad and followed a wagon trail to the base of a hill. Emma in the meantime ran to Clifford who lay strangling on the ground. She pulled his tongue from the cut in his lower jaw and helped to him feet. Still defiant, he waved a bloody fist and shouting in the direction of the departed Confederates.

Approximately two miles south of the farm house, the Confederates took cover in a stand of scrub brush at the base of a hill where on its crest stood a sprawling oak tree of considerable size. Captain Clarkson ordered Private Elam up the hill to keep a lookout for Federal troops. Grumbling, the Private walked up the hill and climbed upon a low hanging limb. He reasoned there would be little food for him after mouthing off to the Captain.

Below the hill, somewhere in the cover of brush, a fire was started and a small kettle placed over it and filled with water. Several large ears of corn, shuck and all were placed in the water and the men settled back to wait, hungrily anticipating the feast of corn, bread and fruit. Still grumbling, Private Josh Elam sat gazing out over the hill toward the town of Plad. He removed the battered corn cob pipe from a pocket, tamped a piece of twist tobacco into the bowl and lit it, sighing contentedly.

The small village of Plad appeared hazy in the distance, but Elam could see the store and smoke rising from its chimney. Two women were standing near a buggy and only one other horse stood tied in front of the building. A tranquil scene posing no danger for the moment to the Rebels and Elam lay back on the limb to enjoy the pipe.

Meanwhile below the tree in the camp of the Fifth Missouri, the fragrant aroma of boiling corn wafted from the brush. Insignificant, or so it seemed, wisps of green wood smoke dissipated rather quickly over the camp. The men of the Fifth lounged about on the ground, smoking and talking. Captain Clarkson in the company of Sergeant Willard Howe discussed which road would be best to take to Springfield. Their orders were to rendezvous with the rest of the outfit near Wilson Creek to join other Confederate forces that would attempt to take the town of Springfield.

"We have to leave in an hour Will, in order to make it to Wilson Creek in time," said the Captain. "We'll head south on the Lebanon, Fort Scott road, then west on the Handly road and south again cross country."

"That sounds right to me," Willard replied. "The horses and the men needed this rest and a chance to eat some good food. Are you going to let Private Elam come down to eat?"

"Heck yes," answered Clarkson. "I just wanted him to think about mouthing off to me back up the road. He's a good soldier, a bit head strong though."

After finishing the pipe, private Elam, weary of the long night's ride, settled back against the old tree and began dozing. The sun had risen well over the horizon, clearing the sky of night fog. The drone of a bumble bee lured him deeper into an unguarded state of drowsiness. Staring blankly down at the ground, he did not see a small group of Union soldiers leave the road across from the Plad store into the brush.

Captain John Dugan and seven men of the Eighth Missouri Home Guard had seen smoke rising above the trees a short distance northeast of Woodhill, another small town about a mile from Plad. After reaching Plad they proceeded on with great caution and headed due north toward the smoke.

Captain Dugan upon reaching a large grove of walnut trees near the western edge of Plad dispatched two men on foot to scout ahead and find the source of the smoke. The rest secured the horses and sat down to wait.

"I can smell corn a cooking," one soldier said.

"Yeah I was thinking the same thing," replied another.

"You boys keep your thoughts to yourselves," cautioned the Captain. "An old man further east of us reported that at least twenty Rebs came in on him and his wife early this morning. He said they roughed him up and cut him with a knife and then stole a basket of corn, some bread and jars of fruit. They may be long gone, but until we find out for sure, keep as quite as possible."

Approximately thirty minutes later the scouts returned, excited by what they had discovered.

"Captain," Private Dan Stafford said, trying to catch his breath. "There are at least twenty and maybe more rebels camped in a shallow hollow about a half a mile from here. The brush is very thick there, but we could see they were cooking something in a kettle. It smelled like corn. We didn't see a sentry, but that don't mean they ain't one."

"We're badly outnumbered, but we can't just turn tail and run," Captain Dugan said. "We'll leave the horses with Jim and proceed on foot and try to get close enough to ambush them and at least take out a few. Go in pairs in a line across the hill here. Keep in sight of one another and don't shoot unless you have to. I want to get very close to them."

Two by two the six men fanned out through the trees and brush and soon approached the clearing where private Elam sat in the oak tree. No one in the Union group had yet to see the Confederate soldier.

Two men of Dugan's group nearest the oak tree darted from the brush intending to take cover there, awakening Elam with sounds of their footsteps.

Elam, drawing his sidearm, caught the glimpse of Union Blue darting from the brush. "Captain, Captain, Yankees are coming," he yelled.

Immediately shots rang out from the brush behind Elam, one nicking him in the right arm. The impact sent him reeling back over the limb, tearing the revolver from his hand. The other two shots slammed into the tree over his head. Terrified, he jumped from the tree landing close to a Mississippi musket lying on the ground. Snatching up the musket, thumbing the hammer back with his left hand, Elam brought the heavy rifle up. Too frightened to sight down the barrel, he brought it to bear on a union man running toward him only to discover it was not capped. Cursing, he plunged a bloody hand into a pocket of his pants and came out with a cap. Fumbling, cursing he finally managed to cap the weapon, but too late.

A fifty eight Minnie ball stuck him in the stomach, knocking him on his back. The Mississippi musket roared, but brought down only a scattering of leaves. Screaming, Elam tried to sit up and recover his rifle, but could not and rolled over on his stomach. Another Minnie ball smashed into the ground near his head and yet another hit him in the right leg. Groaning, he went limp, unaware of Union soldiers running past the tree. A skirmish followed as the Union forces cut loose on the men below.

Unwilling to surrender or to fight, Captain Clarkson ordered the men to retreat into the brush. With Minnie balls tearing up the brush around them, the Confederates ran blindly across the rough terrain to where their horses stood tied, leaving behind the precious corn, bread and jars of fruit. Within minutes the shadowy grey images of the Fifth Missouri faded from view and the barrage of gunfire ceased. Miraculously the kettle containing the corn stood intact along with the rest of the food and assortment of gear left behind by the retreating Rebs.

Silence fell upon the encampment and hillside below the oak tree. Not even a breeze stirred as the Union soldiers waited for one last shot. Moments later the camp was secured and in the possession of Dugan's men. The pot of boiling corn was lifted from the fire and the corn placed in a gunny sack. The rest of the food was placed in another sack and the gear left behind thrown on the fire or rendered useless.

Captain Dugan not relishing further confrontation with the larger force they had just routed headed up the hill past the oak where Private Elam lay. They quickly mounted their steeds and without further delay rode southwest toward the county seat of Buffalo, Missouri.

A blue jay calling nearby brought Private Elam to a painful, bewildered consciousness that intensified when he tried to sit up and then he remembered. The realization he'd been wounded appeared not to affect him as much as the musket lying beyond his reach. The blood soaked soil around him had already attracted several flies buzzing noisily about his face. He managed to roll over a couple of times out of the bloody mud and pulled the weapon to his side. His only thought at the moment was to load the rifle, but sitting up was especially painful and after a couple attempts sagged back on the ground. He lay for a time clinching his teeth, mustering all the strength left in his body. Fearing the Yankees were still around, grunting, he sat up swaying from side to side. Pulling the ramrod free, he poured powder down the barrel, dropped in a ball and with the musket wedged against his left foot, drove powder and ball firmly into place. One by one he dropped caps into the grass and after the fourth try pressed one down on the nipple.

The effort had drained him and fighting unconsciousness threatening to send him to the ground found an inner strength deep inside, an unfaltering genetic trait of Tennessee heritage. Lifting hooded eyes he spied a small hickory tree standing several feet on down the slope where he would have a view of the camp. Slowly rising to his feet, using the musket as a staff, hobbled down the hill, crying out piteously. Drooling, blinded by sweat he managed to get to the tree. Dropping the musket, he hooked an arm around the tree and slid to the ground. Lifting his head, vision blurred now, he peered into the abandoned camp.

"Captain." He called out. "Hey you guys I need help. Hurry before them Yankees come again. I'm sorry I didn't let you know sooner. Hey Captain I can still ride, bring my horse up here."

Elam could no longer hold his head up and lay it against the tree. Reaching out he pulled the musket up over one leg. "Lord." he whispered. "Please let Ma know what happened to me."

Late that afternoon shadows had all but covered the hill where Private Josh Elam sat still clutching the musket. Vigilant even in death the eyes stared blankly down the hill to where smoke drifted up from the embers of a camp fire.

Not long before sunset several stealthy figures darted from the brush and then slowly made their way up the hill.

Captain Clarkson and six other men stopped when they came to the lifeless body of Elam. They solemnly removed their hats. All stepping closer to the fallen soldier and they bowed their heads.

"My God, Captain, said one man brokenly. "He died watching over us."

Nodding, the Captain knelt by Elam. "I reckon he did," he whispered. "Let's get him buried, it's too risky to be here and we're already late and we got a long way to travel before morning. The battle of Wilson Creek ain't gonna wait on us."

"Did you know the Private well Captain?" asked a man.

"Yeah I reckon I did," he replied. "He was my first cousin on my mother's side. We grew up together over on the Osage Fork River."

"You sure were tough on him," said a lad standing behind the Captain.

"Yes I reckon I was and I'm sorry about that," he answered. "I promised his ma I would take care of the boy and tried to make a good soldier of him."

“I reckon you did Sir,” replied the man. “He was a bit headstrong but that ain’t what got him killed. Too many Yankees ganged upon him. He’s shot to pieces.”

“What do you reckon them Yanks were doing this far south?” asked another man.

“I don’t know but it might have to do with a larger bunch of them seen around Springfield. Word has it they are going to try and defend the city.”

“Where do you want Elam buried Captain?’ asked Sergeant Howe, pressing a hand to his eyes.

“On up the hill under the shade of that big oak tree,” he answered. “Carl you and Tom fetch that chunk of limestone we sat on in camp and cut in it the best you can his name and date of birth. The rest of us will dig a hole. Maybe someday I’ll bring his ma here with a better marker. That boy ain’t gonna be forgotten if I have anything to say about it.”

THE END

Country Roads

In the beginning as man began to leave the safety of trees and high bluff caves to go in search of more abundant food sources the roads were waiting. They were not paved, or neatly graveled, but there nevertheless to lead them into the future. Migration trails of animals were perhaps the first attempt at traveling beyond the places of man's origin. Narrow traces fraught with danger lead humankind to new discoveries where along the way the trails were widened, branched off from one location to another. Curious adventurous souls increasingly discontented kept moving toward distant horizons, leaving behind new cultures and life ways to build along the infant roads.

Somewhere along one of those ancient trails, man discovered a god, perhaps while witnessing lighting striking a tree, marveling at the succulent taste of burnt animal flesh, but remembering the awesome destructive power. There were others and the wrath of the gods, fire, wind and rain to name but a few would soon dominate the spiritual aspect of mankind. Fearing these gods they set about building shrines along the roads. Blood, the essence of life was offered to appease the gods, was and still is in some instances a major life way of man. Ancient temples still remain on earth, many are crumbling ruins a reminder of cultures born along a road.

The gods still reign supreme, but their faces have changed and I know of no road that does not lead to a place of worship. The Old Testament is but one of the written books that have spawned religious doctrines over many thousands of years. It is doubtful man will ever reconcile the differences that began separating him since the dawn of time along one of those narrow roads. I am certain; however, when man leaves the planet to follow the stars, children will be born free of earth to become children of the universe and perhaps without bias, focusing at last on the magnificent essence of the never ending creation around them and most important accept God as one.

The birth of country roads in America that ultimately evolved rather quickly into many of the super highways of this land began along the narrow, leafy trails used by the Indians.

Traces so narrow they afforded little room to maneuver were rapidly widened with broad axe and cross cut saw. From those crooked roads that spread like spider webs across Europe, spawning a diversity of humans, cultures, religious dogmas, greed and power compelled a people to invade the Americas. In a relative short time a tidal wave of humanity sought out the multitude of trails across a wilderness as mysterious as the Garden of Eden.

History of course reveals catastrophic changes began the entire length and breadth of the Americas. The invasion of white folks brought about the displacement and or destruction of old cultures in America. Fragile at best theses life ways that had existed for thousands of years fell like wheat before a scythe. They, the Europeans representing great and powerful cultures ultimately and perhaps unintentionally built nations over the ruins of other cultures.

The Osage Indians, inhabitants of the Niangua River basin located in southwest Missouri, were of Siouan stock and giants in comparison to other Native Americans. Most were six foot in height, including the women and it was not unusual to find a man who stood seven feet.

Strength, unity, strict family and moral values was a steadfast life way for these gentle giants of the Ozarks. They were seldom challenged by other tribes and lived in relative peace. The Osage cultivated maze, squash, gathered berries, nuts and seeds and hunted wild game that flourished abundantly within the Niangua River basin.

It is quite possible the lodge fires burned far into the night when at last word came of white men invading the outlying areas of their domain on a trail leading in. White men with hairy faces, who stank like creatures that dwell in caves and rode strange four legged beasts, followed the trail widening it as they came closer. But simple curiosity may have prevailed and leaving the confines of their camps, the Osage stood innocently at trail's edge gaping at the possession arriving, marking the beginning of their end to a life of freedom.

I once knew an old man of Siouan stock, stubbornly holding on to the old ways. He knew at a glance the healing plants and could sense danger in summer storms.

He unashamedly grieved for the many aspects of nature that have fallen before the relentless forces of progress.

Wide set dark eyes never wavered when speaking of his convictions and God, and although he was not a militant man, the strength of his Indian heritage was uncompromising. The old man teased me with many secrets and stories, all of ancient origin and a part of the Niangua River legacy.

Several years ago while on a float trip down the Osage Fork River, I came upon a large cave located beneath a high stone shelf. I could see a narrow path leading from the bank up the steep incline and being a curious soul decided to have a look around. When I arrived at the cave entrance I was astounded by the size of it. It stood towering above me at least twenty five feet and approximately one hundred feet in width. Sadly I quickly discovered other people had been there before me. Pot hunters had left great holes in the floor, some measuring at least twelve feet deep and as wide. Bones lay everywhere and could be seen sticking out of the walls of the excavations. Worst of all many of the bones were human skeletal remains. Broken skulls lay in the bottom of the pits and along the rims of the digs. Incomplete flint tools lay about, along with earthen potshards. The scene was one of complete devastation. Lost forever was knowledge pertaining to the early inhabitants of the mighty cave.

To my right I could see a well worn path or trail snaking up the bluff. I'm certain it was used by these inconsiderate people following it to the cave to dig for the very essence of a people that lived in the cave thousands of years before. I cannot express my true feelings as I wandered about the site. I came upon a trash dump lying near one outer edge of the entrance. It contained beer and soda cans, including other related debris. I quickly discovered by kicking aside many of the cans that the area beneath them was about the only place outside and inside the massive cave not disturbed.

Dropping to my knees I feverishly began clearing a portion of the area to have a closer look. Time was important for I needed to be on my way and considering the chance that I might encounter the pot hunters I worked as quickly as I could. The soil beneath the trash heap, like the rest of the cave site was powder dry and armed only with a stout stick I easily penetrated the dirt sending up a cloud of dust.

Within a half hour I had cleared a small hole to a depth of approximately eighteen inches discovering the remains of a hide still containing hair. Choking a bit on the dust swirling around me, I continued and soon unearthed a very large human skull, or should say the remains of a mummified human head. Hair, nose lips and face were intact, attached to a torso clothed in a lager piece of the hide and attached to it two arms with the hands folded over the chest, nearly perfectly preserved.

I gave up all pretense of watching my back and worrying about the time and set about trying to unearth as much of the upper part of the remains as I could. Three arrow shafts containing stone points were located lying next to the left side of the deceased. A large earthen bowl lay upside on its chest. I soon discovered the remains were of a man, a very large fellow. The robe or hide that shrouded the man extended to his feet.

By this time my hands were a mess, cut and bleeding and the dust about me becoming more than I could handle. From one of my pockets I removed a small measuring tape and discovered the man was at least seven feet six inches long.

Stepping away from the site I waited until much of the dust had settled and knelt by this ancient Indian, more than likely an Osage. I gently touched the gnarled, boney hands and looked down into the inanimate face. The tall man would have been a magnificent creature and even in death an unforgettable sight. Several moments later I replaced the soil, adding stones and lastly put back all the cans and debris. I never returned to the cave where the Tall One lies and have often wondered if he is still there.

Most of the old trails that once meandered across America have long since faded and are forgotten, but of those that did not slip into infinity, a few would become the instruments by which to channel Indians from their ancestral lands to reservations.

In the late winter of 1838, ragged caravans of Cherokees began a forced march to Oklahoma. Many of these groups of Indians passed through Missouri along the Trail of Tears on quite country roads that left behind orphaned children along with men and women too sick to travel. Several died, but many did not and today the Cherokee blood flows through the veins of hundreds of descendants of settlers along the Trail of Tears.

To understand an occurrence of such magnitude, yet most certainly not to condone it, all aspects leading up to the final removal of the Cherokee people scattered across the south and east of this nation should be noted.

Unscrupulous land speculators and politicians with visionary eyes focused on the constant wave of humanity arriving from Europe, traveling the roads demanding land to settle on, reeked of great potential wealth for theses individuals. The discovery of gold in Georgia and surrounding area only fueled the intent to rid the land of the Cherokee. It did not matter that these Native Americans had complied with all requirements set down by the government. The Cherokee believed until the last hour so to speak that the land was lawfully theirs.

The European immigrants had money to spend and were impatient to find land to settle in their new found homeland. Few if any of the men who wanted the Cherokee removed were not concerned how the land would be taken. There were some people who objected to the impending relocation of the Cherokee Nation, recognizing it as an act of piracy. Among those opposing the act were John Quincy Adams, Daniel Webster, Henry Clay and Dave Crocket. Their valiant efforts to stop the relocation along the roads leading to Oklahoma would be in vain.

The treaty with the Cherokees was cast aside and Federal laws changed and with the last of obstacles pushed aside, an invasion into the Land of the Cherokee began. The roads were suddenly alive with soldiers and the Indians suffered quick defeat, their land confiscated, their livestock either slaughtered or stolen. The people were placed in stockades and the horrendous nightmare began along unsuspecting country roads.

Approximately one thousand Cherokee men, women and children, some of mixed race were the first to begin a perilous journey along the distant roads. Several Indians aided by white friends and relatives fled along the trails and secondary roads into the Smokey Mountains. Hundreds died and were buried near the road sides, some escaped and several pregnant women were allowed to be cared for in the homes of kind people. An unknown number of Cherokee women became wives of white male settlers.

The many rivers that lay before the Indians on the Trail of Tears including the Niangua were at times swollen with flood waters near freezing temperatures. Wagons containing the refuges were often swept off the muddy roads. Those that survived staggered ashore exhausted, numbed by the cold and forced to continue along the roads that took them away from their homes and life ways.

The Trail of Tears passed through Georgia, Alabama, Illinois, Missouri and Arkansas, leaving behind a grim legacy along those scenic, seemly peaceful wandering roads.

Perhaps the most colorful and memorable legacies left along America's roads of old, carried from England, Ireland, Scotland, Germany, France and Africa was the music. The instruments brought with the white settlers and slaves of Africa varied in flavor and construction, from the very finest to the most primitive, but all represented the music of the time.

The Mountain banjo is my favorite and was the product of the early settlers of this country. In an era when music was about the only meaningful pass time, it rang out along the roads in the deep Southland, carried westward on the deeply rutted wagon trails to the sod houses of Kansas. Long before Sears, Roebuck and Company came out with a mass produced fretted banjo, the Mountain Banjo had become a legendary aspect of Americana.

The Mountain Banjo was born of the innovative spirit of the Irish, Scottish, English and African. The instrument played its way westward on the backs of buckskinners, accompanied families along the often perilous roads across deserts and High Mountain passes and eased the loneliness in the many forts standing at trail's end. Most folks had time to play, sing and dance whether they had time to do anything else. The songs they sang and played often against the backdrop of a wilderness where the trails of Indians were the only way in or out, reflected their hardships, joys and individual family values.

Black Americans, held in bondage, contributed much to the gospel sound of this country, often accompanied by a banjo constructed from whatever material at hand. Deeply entwined are the words of hope and the twang of a mountain banjo that could be heard along the roads in the shadows of magnificent plantations homes.

The roots of country music are deeply embedded in America, and seldom heard anymore, but there are a few people who have not lost track of the early sounds of our heritage music. You can find them along dusty roads in the Deep South, northward into Arkansas, or along the Niangua River basin, still singing the prettiest songs you ever heard. Songs like Sally Gooden, Devil's Dream, and Waltz of the Indian, Leather Britches, and bringing folks together along the country roads and settlements of old.

Country roads of the early years of this nation led armies into battle and later, whether victorious or defeated, returned thousands of weary men to their homes. James Wright, a Confederate Sergeant Major, upon his surrender at the close of the Civil War, walked from Shreveport Louisiana, approximately 300 hundred miles along war scarred country roads to his home in Kingston Arkansas. The Trail of Tears will remain a graphic reminder in the pages of history to the greed and corruption that forced the Cherokee from their land on a road of devastation. Country roads united a nation as they cut through the heart of a people who stood in the way.

Unlike some of the super highways of this land that are stained with the blood of war and discriminatory events, country roads offer those who travel them, quite memories, tree shrouded passage to the crest of a hill where the sunset lingers beneath clouds aflame with its waning light, the fragrance of new mown hay, the song of a mourning dove or the fleeting glimpse of a wily coyote disappearing into the brush. Country roads still meander past old cemeteries, forgotten homestead sites, sagging one room school buildings and leaning outhouses peeking out from their cover of plum thickets and ivy vines. Many of the country roads of the present ford creeks and rivers much as they did in the early years across low water slabs of concrete or shallow riffles. Country roads have been left to wander into the deep hollows, canyons, high ridges and rolling prairies of a nation thrust into the Twenty-first Century.

The maintenance of country roads is often ignored or conspicuously done just before an election. Even the material that is used to cover the surface of most of these old roads has not changed. River or creek gravel covers many of them and it is not uncommon to find in it broken stone tools of another people who once traveled along the trace.

I have stood many times on a high ridge too far from home to seek shelter watching a summer storm rise above the horizon or watched the sun slip out of sight below the burning embers of day and welcomed the sunrise after a long cold night in a cave. It is in these moments that I reflect best on my state of existence and renew my enthusiasm for life and take note of my dreams. I am seldom content with the present and anxious to see where another road will lead me. The horizon is farther than I shall ever go, yet I have stood where few of my kind have been, but I am pleased for if I should travel to its limit, no longer would I dream. Perhaps there will be a time when my spirit will not need a road, but will ride the wind to the highest peak, or dance with the spring in a green meadow or gently bring about the first smile to an infant.

I would rather walk along the edge of a field of flowers, leaving not a trace of my presence for fear of returning someday to find a road. I would rather sit on the bank of a river at twilight with my hound, drinking camp coffee, than be in the midsts of a midnight crowd of people drinking wine. John and I rode the river many times beneath summer skies, sharing our dreams, our souls and love of the land. "Good-by John."

Chance encounters, I am certain have at times been instrumental in shaping one's future. Consequential events that should not be ignored, for they are not unlike the random dropping of seeds by the wind far from their places of origin, or just beyond the next hill; a chance encounter at the end of a road, a juncture in my life where a beautiful, dark haired, green eyed young woman unknowingly awaited my arrival.

Many country roads are concealed beneath canopies of old growth trees and one in particular that follows the east bank of Indian Creek deep in the Missouri Ozarks, offered quite seclusion where a '48 Plymouth and its two young lovers often sat beneath a moonlit sky and dreamed of tomorrow. This country road is but one of many where ghosts walk the night, where high sentinels of weathered limestone bluffs tower above the tree line and are the places where secrets are kept within the dismal confines of caves. These country roads are where solitude can be found, where high above their dusty traces, buzzards ride the wind, lingering for a time after the first light of dawn. The journey to distant horizons continues across old Indian lands that still hold many secrets yet to be discovered.

IT" TIME TO HEAD HOME.
ADIOS.

Author's Notes

A stranger arrived in London Smoke, Missouri early one day in the latter part of 1890 looking for a particular spring. Most folks in those days were wary of strangers and the people in London Smoke were no exception, but gave the man the information he requested. It was later noted, a large stone had been moved aside near the spring and laying in the depression was a rusted cap lock Colt revolver and the remnant of a leather pouch, containing a single twenty dollar gold piece.

Stories abound about the stranger, but they are only stories, folktales, bearing only a grain of truth. I have listened to most of these tales and the Stranger rides again in my book of the Stranger in London Smoke.

"Tiddleson," or so said my son at the age of eight years was observed coming out of an old rusty lard can that lay in a cedar glade. "Dad," he exclaimed, "the feller was no taller than a dandelion stem!"

To most folks the boy's revelation was a bit far fetched, but I found the tale quite interesting and so Tiddleson, Son of Tiddle came to be in a larger-than-life novel of the Amicus People depicting their precarious journey from Ireland to the Ozarks and the struggle to survive in a land dominated by the crushing civilization of larger humans.

The story combines fantasy, adventurous exploits and strong willed little people who dwell in the Missouri Ozarks.

Along with the above mentioned are more stories waiting in the wings, such as, "Ronnie and Jessie and the "Imitators."

Ronnie